Hearts *racing*.
Blood *pumping*.
Pulses *accelerating*.

*Falling in love can be a blur...
especially at 180 mph!*

So if you crave the thrill of the chase—on and off the track—you'll love

FULL THROTTLE
by Wendy Etherington!

Ever since she'd come back to work with her father this year, the tension between her and Kane had been building. She wondered when—not if—it would explode.

Their relationship in high school had been just as volatile. Full of heat and conflict, frustration and arguments.

But very passionate.

The team needed that fever now. They needed the old Kane, not the one who'd somehow gotten buried over the years under the corporate endorsement man. They didn't need the man who moved to the side and let drivers pass when he should hold his position. Or the man who accepted sixth place when he should go for the win. He'd somehow lost his racing fire.

Personally, though, she had to be careful about passion. She'd been hired to stoke some new life into Kane and the team. But how did she pour gasoline on a fire and not get burned again?

she said finally. "You want this championship. You need it.

Dear Reader,

To say I've had a great time writing this book would be a ridiculous understatement.

I pretty much spend my days at my laptop writing (and when my kids get home from school, I run the dance/gymnastics taxi service), so my down time is important for recharging my creative batteries. I fill that time with NASCAR racing.

As a kid growing up in Birmingham, I remember my dad watching the Alabama Gang, Harry Gant, Dale Earnhardt and Richard Petty. But I didn't become a true fan until I was an adult. I've been crazy about racing for more than a decade now, and I seem to grow steadily more supportive (and sorta obsessed) every season.

A lot of years have passed since the first race I attended in the spring of 1994 in Atlanta, since I picked out my first driver to follow and since those cars roared down the straightaway for the first time, live, seemingly just for me. I was hooked for life.

I hope my passion for the sport comes through in Kane and Lexie's story. If you're not already a fan, I hope you become one. If you are, then you're already a friend.

I'd love to hear from you (though I'm unavailable most Sunday afternoons). You can contact me through my Web site, www.wendyetherington.com, or through regular mail at P.O. Box 3016, Irmo, SC 29063.

Let's go racing!

Wendy Etherington

///////// NASCAR®

FULL THROTTLE

Wendy Etherington

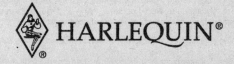

HARLEQUIN®

TORONTO • NEW YORK • LONDON
AMSTERDAM • PARIS • SYDNEY • HAMBURG
STOCKHOLM • ATHENS • TOKYO • MILAN • MADRID
PRAGUE • WARSAW • BUDAPEST • AUCKLAND

ISBN-13: 978-0-373-21773-1
ISBN-10:   0-373-21773-0

FULL THROTTLE

WENDY ETHERINGTON

was born and raised in the deep South—and she has the fried chicken recipes and NASCAR ticket stubs to prove it. Though a voracious reader since childhood, she spent much of her professional life in business and computer pursuits. Finally giving in to those creative impulses, she began writing, and in 1999 she sold her first book.

She has been a finalist for many awards—including the Booksellers' Best Award and several *Romantic Times BOOKreviews* awards. In 2006 she was honored by Georgia Romance Writers as the winner of the Maggie Award.

She writes full-time (when she's not watching racing) from her home in South Carolina, where she lives with her husband and two daughters.

To Liz Allison,
whose strength and friendship is always inspiring.

CHAPTER ONE

"TROUBLE, TURN TWO. Go high, go high."

Kane Jackson saw only smoke through his windshield, but he responded instinctively to his spotter's instructions. Less than a second later, a red, white and blue car slid past the left side of his race car. "The Hatchet?"

"Yeah," Kane's crew chief, Harry Mercer, responded, his tone flat. "He's talking. Not hurt."

"Good." On both counts, he thought, very aware that millions of people via online simulcasts could hear every word he said into his radio. Privately Kane couldn't deny his sense of relief that the points leader for the NASCAR NEXTEL Cup Championship, Patrick "The Hatchet" Williams was probably done for the day. Kane had a tricky road to make the top ten—The Chase as it had been dubbed by NASCAR—and Pat was a semifriend, but definitely the competition.

Obstacles are just one smart move away from the path to greatness.

His father's words whispered through his brain so suddenly he could swear the man himself sat in the passenger's seat where there was in reality nothing but emptiness and part of the roll cage. He tried to shake off the insecurity that thoughts of his father always brought about.

He'd never measure up to "The Legend." But then nobody could.

Maybe he was stuck in fourteenth place with four races to go until The Chase began, but he was on a roll. His team was pumped. Thanks to the testing sessions, the cars were running better than they had in a long time. Aerodynamic issues had been solved. Camber and tire pressure were adjusted throughout the race. Pit crew motivation was high.

And almost everything good could be attributed not to him, but to Harry and his brilliant daughter, Lexie.

He heard her voice now as the caution flag came out and he prepared to make a critical pit stop. "They're waving the flag at lap one-seven-five. Last stop. Four tires."

"Let's not take any chances," he said. The car was great. Only twenty-five laps to go.

"We wouldn't dream of it," Lexie returned, her tone dry. "We're in sixth. It's a good finish."

"See what you can do with fresh tires. Hold your line."

The tension in her voice was evident. Once, he'd shared in her laughter. Her eyes had sparkled in his presence. These days he saw frustration. Dissatisfaction.

Maybe he'd never measure up with her, either.

"I'll try," he said.

Keeping a close eye on his tachometer, he cruised down pit road at a teeth-grinding forty-five miles per hour, then rolled into his pit box above the neon yellow and red Sonomic Oil flag marked with Number 53.

Wrapping his hands around the wheel, he waited the seeming eternity while his team changed the car's tires. In actuality less than fourteen seconds passed, but in that time he glanced out his window, and even through the thick black netting he could see beyond the pit wall and spot

Lexie—her scowl and her concentration, her small, feminine body seeming somehow familiar and out of place in the racing uniform that matched his own. Lips he'd once had the pleasure of tasting were pursed in concentration.

He shook his head at the distraction and quickly pulled away from the pits, cutting into the line of cars exiting pit road in third place.

"Thirteen point four," Harry said through the headset in his helmet.

"Yeah!" Kane roared back. "Awesome stop, guys." The top ten seemed closer by the second.

Falling in line with the other leaders, he vowed to keep both Lexie and his father out of his mind. The next twenty-five laps were about racing, not relationships. Nearly every minute of the day was about racing, though, which was probably why most of his relationships were in the toilet.

As the green flag waved, he concentrated on taking each turn of the tri-oval of Michigan's track, relief creeping closer as Harry counted down the laps. As the cars roared down the straightaway, he could smell the burning rubber, he could see the fans standing in their seats, each screaming for their driver. He thought he even spotted a few sporting his yellow and red team colors.

You have to earn the fans' respect, son. Winning will make that happen. Fans like winners.

The old man seemed determined to intrude on his peace today. But then, was that different from any other day?

"White flag, white flag."

A grin teased the corners of Kane's mouth. *Twenty-three races down, thirteen to go.*

As he drove out of Turn Two, in his rearview mirror, he saw the Number 86 car overtake the car behind him. When he felt the tap, he barely flinched. He didn't slam his fist against the dash. He didn't cuss. He didn't scream.

But he stopped smiling.

His car's back end wrenched around, spinning and sliding up the track. The field scattered. Tires screeched. Smoke billowed.

"That's Kane Jackson in the Number 53 car on the outside retaining wall," the announcer shouted over the track speakers.

With his car resting against the wall, Kane unhooked the window net to let the safety crew know he was all right, then he bowed his head and started counting to ten to keep the raging fury and disappointment from overtaking him.

Those anger management classes were certainly handy at times.

Before he'd reached nine, the safety crew's truck had pulled alongside him. "You all right, Mr. Jackson?"

His blood roared like the crowd's cheers for the winner, but Kane calmly dragged off his helmet. "I'm fine." He hoisted himself through the window, then gave a quick wave of thanks to the safety guys. Sparing only a glance for his mangled race car, he walked across the track toward the ambulance idling next to the infield grass. At least the required ride to the track medical care center would give him time to get his thoughts and emotions in order before the inevitable media interviews. He wasn't exactly looking forward to facing his team, either.

Even though the wreck hadn't been his fault, he'd lost major ground in his bid to make the top ten. Points couldn't be recovered. The accident would affect everyone on the team. And though Harry and Lexie were their actual leaders, he was the emotional center. It was his name and face plastered all over the team's merchandise. The honor was amazing during the good times, but the responsibility when things went wrong was greater.

The safety crew member turned Kane over to a short, muscled medic, who stood at the back of the ambulance. Smiling briefly, he met Kane's gaze. "Black out?"

"No."

"Dizzy?"

"No."

He directed a pen light into his eyes. "Looks okay. Let's go."

"Mike Streetson pulls his Number 76 Chevrolet into Victory Lane!" the announcer roared.

Kane sat on a gurney. "Streetson held on?"

"Won by four car lengths," the medic said as he followed Kane into the back of the ambulance.

"There's some good news."

Streetson was a self-described grizzled veteran who hadn't won a race in nearly two years and who was too far down in the points race to have a chance to make the top ten. Not only was his win good for Kane's championship bid, but he admired his fellow racer more than just about any man he knew.

The medic sat next to Kane and pressed his fingers against his wrist as they bumped along toward the infield care center. "You're awfully calm after a wild wreck like that."

"I have a low pulse rate."

"Yeah? 'Spect it's genetic." He grinned. "After your daddy threw that winning touchdown in the Super Bowl, he talked to reporters right there on the sidelines. He wasn't even breathin' hard."

Long used to his father's adoring fans, Kane nodded. "Amazing, wasn't he?"

"Retired on top—smart man. And he's still super. Best broadcaster in the business. You play ball?"

Considering the man had just watched him walk away from a stock car crash in front of more than a hundred thousand spectators and millions of TV viewers, Kane had to suppress a start of surprise. "Not since high school."

The medic flushed. "Oh, right."

Poor guy. Couldn't make it, knew he'd never measure up to his father.

Though the words weren't said aloud this time, Kane knew what the medic was thinking. He'd heard—and over-heard—them before. It never occurred to these people that he simply didn't like football. Watching it was fun. Playing it was not. It wasn't until age nineteen that he rose to his present height of six-one and finally developed breadth in his chest and lean, powerful muscles.

Before that he'd been fairly small. In his sophomore year of high school he'd only reached five-eight. He was fit but thin, and not very strong. Weight work with his father's personal trainer had helped only minimally. Diet and private quarterback lessons hadn't made much difference, either. He couldn't run very fast. And though his reflexes were excellent, he didn't scramble well under pressure. Eventually—so Kane had overheard one night during a meeting of his father and his cronies—they all had to face the facts.

Anton Jackson's son didn't have a cannon for an arm. He had a bottle rocket that would never fire.

Kane had shared that revelation with only two people in his life—his girlfriend, Lexie Mercer, and his best friend and the star receiver of his high school football team, James Peterson. To take his mind off his troubles, James and Lexie took Kane to his first stock car race near their hometown of Mooresville, North Carolina.

The rest, as they say, is history.

"Well," the medic continued, releasing his wrist. "You look good. We'll have the doc check you out, but I expect he'll let you go quickly."

"Thanks." At least the guy hadn't asked for an autograph.

"Hey, does your dad usually come to the races?" the medic asked, craning his neck to look around as they stepped out of the ambulance.

Kane sighed. "No, he doesn't."

HER HANDS TREMBLING, Lexie Mercer mounted the stairs to the Hollister Racing company jet. Though she'd been calm when she assured owner Bob Hollister that she'd get the team back on track for Bristol next Saturday night, she was still furious and bitterly disappointed by Kane's finish in the race.

Half a lap. Half a damn lap.

It was frustrating beyond words, and only made the pressure of an already stressful job jump up another notch. Careers and millions of dollars were at stake. As car chief, she was already a woman in a male-dominated world. How many of those men would love to have her position with a successful team like Hollister?

While her father's role as crew chief made him, well, the *chief* of the entire team, it was up to her to see that his plans and orders were carried out, to keep the crew on task, to supervise the technicians and engineers and make sure the car for the next race would fare better.

She got the praise when the car and team performed well, and she felt her boss's disapproval when one or both didn't. The fact that her boss was her father added a whole new level of anxiety.

Still, it fell to all of them—her, her father and Kane— to take charge of recovery and moving forward. Back home at the shop, they had to face the team members who didn't travel with the team. They had to overcome the emotional low of not finishing the race. They had to examine the wrecked vehicle and see what parts could be salvaged.

Most of all, they *had* to get into the top ten.

The first person she saw on the plane was James Peterson, Kane's best friend and manager. His nearly shoulder-length, shaggy blond hair framing his handsome face, he was bent over, clicking beer bottles with Kane, who, bravely, sat in the front row, so he would have to face each person on his team as they walked by him to take their own seat.

She'd admire him more if she wasn't so furious with him.

She exchanged a look with James, who approached with his ought-to-be-outlawed killer grin, then glided past her, heading toward the exit. "Go easy," he muttered.

She glared at his retreating back, seeing no reason for leniency. Something had to change on this team. And Kane Jackson better be prepared to transform himself ASAP.

Thankful the plane was deserted except for the flight crew, she dropped into the seat next to her driver, who, during the TV interview following the race, had actually shrugged and said, "Oh, well" in response to his wreck. "'Oh, well'?"

"Rookies cause wrecks sometimes. He misjudged the passing distance and got into me. He apologized."

She rolled her eyes. "'Oh, well'?"

He glanced at her at last, and the force of those bright-blue eyes made her heart flutter ridiculously. "I had to tell the media something."

"Something with a bit more force and passion would be welcomed."

"Passion, huh?"

Too late, she realized the door she'd opened. "You know what I mean."

He grinned. "Do I?"

She felt the heat from his body and his stare. *That's old and finished,* she tried to tell herself. But with little conviction. Ever since she'd left the Research and Development division of Hollister Racing and come back to work with her father this year, the tension between her and Kane had been building. She wondered when—not if—it would explode.

Their relationship in high school had been just as volatile. Full of heat and conflict, frustration and arguments.

But very passionate.

The team needed that fever now. They needed the old Kane, not the one who'd somehow gotten buried over the years under the corporate endorsement man. They didn't need the man who moved to the side and let drivers pass when he should hold his position. Or the man who accepted sixth place when he should go for the win. The man who'd been trying so desperately all his life to fulfill his image of perfection, he'd somehow lost his racing fire.

Personally, though, she had to be careful about passion. She'd been hired to stoke some new life into Kane and the team. But how did she pour gasoline on a fire and not get burned again?

If she could get past his security team, masseuse, personal trainer, manager and accountant, she was going to kick Anton Jackson's butt when they got home. This "oh, well" version of the once-hot-blooded Kane could be laid right at Anton's feet. He couldn't turn his boy into a mini football version of himself, and he didn't approve of Kane's racing, so he chose to focus on his son's media image rather than his driving.

Anton sent Kane on endless autographing jaunts that crisscrossed the country. He'd forced him into anger management classes. He had reporters follow Kane around as he visited the children's cancer center his charity helped fund, even though Kane had always kept his philanthropic efforts private.

His constant interference and criticism had taken its toll on Kane, draining him of his personality. His confidence suffered. His driving became too cautious. He'd lost his will to win.

"There's always next week," Kane said in that calm tone she'd come to hate.

"There aren't that many next weeks."

Kane raised his eyebrows. "No kidding?"

"Don't be a smart—"

He waggled his finger. "Watch that language, Miss Mercer. NASCAR wouldn't be pleased."

"I'm not worried about NASCAR. I'm worried about you."

"I'm touched."

"Dammit, Kane, wake up! That rookie screwed up big. This could cost us The Chase."

"He's a *rookie,* Lexie. It happens."

"It can't happen to us. We can't afford it."

His eyes went frosty. His jaw tensed.

Come on…yell at me. Tell me to go to hell, she thought.

"We'll do better next week."

She bowed her head. "Sure we will."

He slid his fingers along her jaw. "Chin up, L—"

She jerked back. Her skin tingled where he'd touched her. Her heart pounded as they stared at each other.

Dear God, why him?

The past washed over her as if a minute had passed instead of a decade. She recalled frantic groping in the backs of cars, private smiles and notes in geometry, sitting in the empty grandstands with a bottle of champagne, Kane next to her, unable to leave the scene of his first win.

But she also remembered shouts and tears, Kane leaving her at the homecoming dance, so he could sneak out to the garage at James's grandfather's house where they kept the race car they were secretly building. She'd introduced him to racing—and quickly fallen into second place in his heart.

A calmer, gentler Kane would be different, her traitorous heart whispered.

For her, maybe. But not for her race team.

Confused and frustrated, she rose. "We have to win."

He set his beer bottle aside and stood next to her. "You think I don't know that?"

"I mean, that's what it's going to take—finishing in the top five for the next three races and winning at least one of them. If Pat hadn't wrecked…well, it would be a lot worse. We can still make it. We just can't have any more mistakes."

"I didn't make a mistake today."

"I didn't say you did. I'm just telling you what we're dealing with."

"No problem."

The flare of attraction in his eyes turned to anger. Something about that moment when they'd looked at each other had set him off. Maybe he was struggling with his own memories. Maybe he was frustrated and tired. Or maybe…maybe he was finally fed up with swallowing his emotions.

"If it's no problem, why haven't we done it?"

"You tell me. You set up the cars."

"There's nothing wrong with my setups."

"There's nothing wrong with my driving. We won at Charlotte back in May, remember?"

"Oh, right." She smirked. "It was so long ago I forgot." She watched in fascination as his mouth thinned to a furious line. She could almost hear him start his count to ten.

Naturally, she wasn't letting him get past five.

"How about I call over to Bristol and tell them to go ahead and engrave your name on the trophy? Or maybe you're the next Petty or Earnhardt, and they'll name a grandstand after you."

"Stop it, Lexie," he said in a barely controlled whisper.

Maybe she'd feel guilty later for pushing him over the edge. But she didn't think so. "While you're doing all that winning, you can do the setups yourself, too."

He leaned close to her face. "Why won't you let me touch you?"

"I—*what?*" She stepped back.

He jabbed a finger at the seats they'd just vacated. "You jerked away from me like I'd hit you."

"I was just… It was nothing. I was…surprised. It's been a long day."

"So you thought you'd pick a fight."

She swallowed, struggling between peace and honesty. Honesty won, of course. "I don't like watching you struggle." She pinned him with a glare. "Or lose."

"You think I do?"

"I think you're willing to accept less than you should."

"You're wrong." He paused, his gaze sliding down her body almost like a caress and leaving a trail of heat in its wake. "I want it all."

He jerked her against him before she'd had time to even blink. She'd clearly underestimated those lightning-quick reflexes of his. In the next instant he'd cupped her jaw, and his mouth had captured hers. Frustration and anger poured from him in waves, and he channeled that emotion into his kiss. She tried to fight against the warmth that spread through her veins, against the desire overloading her body, against the emotion he always managed to pull from her heart.

She failed thoroughly. She melted in his arms.

For a few stolen moments she dreamed that things could be exactly the way they were years ago and that things could be different, that the future would be an unrealistic combination of the two. She breathed in his familiar scent of sandalwood and pine. She laid her hand over his heart and felt the intoxicating rush of his pulse.

"Well, Kane," said a familiar voice, "you didn't win the trophy, but it looks like you got first prize, anyway."

CHAPTER TWO

KANE JUMPED AWAY from Lexie, his gaze jerking to James, who gestured with his beer bottle. "Is there something you two want to tell me?"

Kane exchanged a guilty, panicked glance with Lexie. "No," they said together.

"No way," Kane added.

Lexie practically ran to the door. "I, uh, I've got to get…something."

James watched her scramble down the stairs, then he turned back to Kane. "Well, that was—" he grinned "—unexpected."

Kane sank back into his seat. He grabbed his beer bottle and rolled the cold glass against his forehead. "Don't start."

James dropped into the seat next to him. "*Me* start? I didn't even hear the call to fire the engine. You guys were halfway around the track before—"

"I've lost it."

"I wouldn't say that. Sure, she's too brainy for her own good. And she can be bossy as hell, but underneath that uniform and ball cap, she's a total babe."

Kane stared at his best friend, the guy he'd built his first car with, the guy who'd caught most of the lousy passes he'd managed to throw on the football field, the guy he'd cheered for at Florida Gator games for nearly three years before his career-ending knee injury, the guy who'd turned down dozens of job offers to manage Kane's life in racing.

And decided he didn't like him very much.

"Babe, huh? That's my girlfriend you're talking about. Have you had a thing for her all this time? You think you can have her for your—"

"*Girlfriend?* Hey, bud, that was years ago. How hard did you hit your head, anyway?"

He hadn't. But he really wanted to now.

"I don't want to talk about it."

"I bet you don't." Sipping his beer, James was silent a moment, then added, "But you'd better get your thoughts together. Harry was nearly on my heels as I came this way."

Lexie's father. His crew chief. The *boss*. What was he going to say? Do? How would he—

He was saying and doing nothing. In fact, the longer *she* was gone, he couldn't remember why he'd felt so panicked. He'd kissed her. Big deal. He'd certainly done that before.

And more.

With a wave of his somewhat shaky hand, he dismissed the past. Like a dieter who'd tasted his first slice of chocolate cake in months, he'd just gorged, there, for a moment or two. He hadn't hit his head, but the wreck had clearly rattled him. He'd been so confident, so upbeat during the race. It was natural to dive after such a disappointing finish. And grabbing Lexie like that had just been an impulse to find something safe and familiar.

Breathing a sigh of relief, he decided his anger management therapist would be proud of his ability to examine his actions. And even without her infamous engineering genius

and computer calculations on car balance and performance,
Lexie would agree with his diagnosis.

He didn't really *want* his car chief. He just wanted…
well, he wanted to win. And Bristol was as good a place
as any. He'd learned to bury his emotions there, to stay
patient and out of trouble. With three NASCAR Busch
Series wins and a NASCAR NEXTEL Cup win last year,
it was one of his best tracks.

He would once again bottle the feelings Lexie had
forced out of him. He'd encourage the guys at the shop and
get under the hood himself if anybody was stuck. He'd hit
the gym hard and catch up on fan club autographs.

He would do all that—after his two-day trip to Cincinnati, where he'd committed to signing autographs for a
model-car collector's club, a sponsor party and fan ques-
tion-and-answer session. Suddenly the week didn't seem
so bright. It seemed full and long. Crowded with people
he didn't know. Whose respect he didn't see how he'd
earned.

*You should feel privileged, son. Do you know how many
guys would trade places with you in a second?*

Hundreds. Maybe thousands.

But the pressure of that idea only made him feel worse.
He'd never measure up.

Voices at the door yanked him from his self-pity. A
group of crew members moved toward him. All of them
had genuine smiles on their faces as they passed.

"Bad break, Kane."

"Another inch or two and who knows?"

"You wanna get that rookie later?"

"We're behind ya, man."

The responsibilities he had weighing on him weren't

any more complex than the ones of his team. The hours they put in and the time away from their families were sacrifices they'd made to build this team. Sacrifices to *him*. They wanted to get behind a winner, to work for a champion. They were tenacious and loyal, but he also knew if he didn't rise to the top, another guy would come along and lure them away with the promise of working on a better team.

"Tough wreck, Kane," Harry said, laying his hand on his shoulder. "You all right?"

Kane looked up and managed a smile. Harry always found the right tone, the right thing to say. How many times had he longed for his own father's unending support? "I'm fine, boss. We'll get 'em next week."

Looking as if he wanted to say more, shadows filled Harry's eyes, then they were gone and he smiled. "Sure we will."

THE NEXT NIGHT Kane walked onto a high school auditorium stage in Cincinnati as he prepared to answer on-air questions for a local radio station, as well as a select live audience of stock car collectors. The applause made him feel vaguely uncomfortable, but he waved at the gathered crowd and hoped he'd meet their expectations.

"So, Kane, how do you like Cincinnati?" the DJ, Brian, asked.

From long experience, Kane answered the question, along with ones about racing and his past with ease. Even when the inevitable came, he didn't flinch from the truth— or at least the portion he felt comfortable expressing.

"Come on now, you're telling me your dad didn't want another Heisman trophy in the house?"

"He did, I guess. But when you're a junior in high school, and you're five-eight, one-forty and slow, there aren't a lot of colleges scrambling for you to lead them to victory."

The crowd laughed as they always did, and he focused on the freedom that had come after that momentous revelation in his life and not what had gone before.

"You traded the Heisman for the NASCAR NEXTEL Cup Championship?"

"Let's hope so."

"And I understand you stole another football great for your team. All-American receiver James Peterson of Florida is your manager."

He looked to the wings of the stage, where Lexie, James and Pete, his front-tire changer and a graduate of the high school where they'd all gathered, stood in silent support. "That's true."

"You also have a female car chief."

Kane's heart gave one hard thump in response. "I do."

Wolf whistles followed, which he could hardly argue against.

"A Duke engineering graduate," Brian added.

"Certainly smarter than me."

He didn't dare look at Lexie, who was no doubt flushing and rolling her eyes, wondering when they could get this whole business over with and talk strategy for Bristol. He hadn't seen her at all before the moment she'd stepped on the plane for this trip. And Pete had sat between them on the way to the auditorium.

The separation was for the best. They needed to get back on their professional track and not let a personal…relapse interfere with this week's race.

"Don't forget Pete," someone in the audience shouted out.

Brian chuckled. "I don't see how we could. In fact, why don't we bring out James, Lexie and Pete? I'm sure our audience has questions for them, too."

The crowd roared at this, and his friends walked out on stage, with James practically dragging Lexie in his wake. Her hair was down for once, brushing her shoulders and framing her face with soft-looking brown waves.

Several more stools were brought out, and Kane found himself sitting between the DJ and Lexie. Their gazes met for a moment as Brian questioned Pete about life on the racing circuit, but Lexie quickly looked away.

Kane fought a wince. Maybe his silence had been a mistake. He hadn't even apologized. He'd justified himself by insisting she'd provoked him—and on purpose. But that didn't excuse his actions. Taking out his frustration on her was uncalled-for. He definitely didn't want her to think it would happen again, or that she was in danger of being grabbed at any moment. They needed to trust and support each other.

As a team, of course. The other…personal stuff, well, that was over. *Way* over.

"So, Lexie," the DJ said as he turned away from Kane, "you're the only female car chief on the circuit. How does it feel being surrounded by guys all the time?"

"Sweaty."

Kane grinned at Lexie's deadpan tone. She always shied away from the spotlight and hated talking to the media, answering "all those stupid questions."

Naturally, everybody laughed at her response, which only caused her frown to deepen. She was no doubt serious.

"But how well do you get along with the team?" Brian persisted. "The track is kind of an odd place to find a woman."

"After the voting booth, it seemed to be the last barrier for us." Silence and a few uneasy chuckles followed this statement. And though Lexie was definitely more comfortable in the garage than on stage, she sensed the tension immediately. "We get along fine, Brian, and I raced go-karts as a kid, so I'm used to guys. And challenges."

"Go-karts," Brian said, glancing down at a piece of paper in his lap. "This was back in California. Your father was your coach and crew chief."

"If you want to call me and my mom the crew."

"She passed away suddenly, and you moved to North Carolina."

Lexie pressed her lips together briefly. "Yes. Dad got an offer to work in stock car racing, I retired from the track and we became part of the NASCAR family." She glanced at Kane and smiled, and even though he knew her joy was for the audience, warmth still spread through his chest. "James and I even took Kane to his first race."

"Again, football's loss is NASCAR's gain."

This time her smile for Kane was filled with genuine warmth. "Oh, yeah."

After a few audience questions, the interview was wrapped up, and Kane slid off the right-hand side of the stage for autographs. A long line of car collectors formed, and he spent the next two hours signing mini plastic versions of his race car and taking photos with fans. A few would undoubtedly wind up on eBay to be resold, but most people seemed to be big fans of his, Hollister Racing or just NASCAR in general.

The kids, in particular, were a blast. They liked to push the cars across the table and make "rrrring" noises. The older ones claimed they, too, would one day be signing autographs; the younger ones were just happy to be part of the excitement.

Kane remembered signings from his own youth, when his father had been the star. When he'd sat on the floor of the stadium media center, pushing toy cars and trucks around on an imaginary track. When the fans had smiled indulgently over a legend's cute kid. Maybe he didn't see the devotion and awe in the eyes of Cincinnati people that his father inspired, but he didn't need it. He was happy making a living at the sport he loved.

Though having legions of fans wouldn't suck.

"Nice job, everybody," James said as they climbed into the rented SUV. "Who's hungry?"

"No burgers," Lexie said. "Let's go somewhere besides the drive-through window."

James, sitting on the bench seat next to Lexie, laid his arm around her shoulders. "As it happens, I made reservations at a charming Italian place just a few blocks away."

Lexie grinned up at James, and Kane clenched his hands into fists. How could she be so easy with James when all Kane managed to do was irritate and annoy her?

"*I* made the reservations," their driver, Stan, reminded them. A race fan and manager at their premier sponsor, Sonomic Oil, he'd volunteered to serve as host and designated driver for their night in Cincinnati. After the last few stressful days, James had decided they all needed a break, so they were spending the night in a hotel.

A relaxing dinner sounded like a dream compared to the upcoming weekend at Bristol. Forty-three drivers, all hell-bent on surviving the grueling half-mile track on a wild Saturday night in front of more than 150,000 fans was an intense experience.

After Kane shoved aside his stupid irritation at James and Lexie, their dinner group was upbeat as they were escorted to their corner booth by the hostess. Over pasta, salad and buttery garlic rolls, they shared stories and talked racing. Kane tried to ignore his tingling hands when Lexie laughed.

What was wrong with him?

They were professional colleagues now. High school was long over. Their relationship didn't extend beyond friendship.

A fact that was cemented when a group of female fans approached their table and asked for his autograph. Showing no signs of resentment, Lexie laughed along with the rest of the group and even volunteered to take their picture with him. After his jealous rumblings all night, Kane felt like an even bigger heel for kissing her yesterday.

At the time, he was sure she'd responded with their old fire, but clearly reading female responses was lost on him unless the woman happened to be pressing a hotel key in his hand—as the blond autograph-seeker was currently doing.

"I'm at the Best Western," she said close to his ear. "Room 242."

He'd had similar experiences before—had even accepted a couple of times early in his career—but he inevitably wondered what the woman really wanted. The pedal-to-the-metal driver on the track? Anton Jackson's son? A signed photo, with a "Thanks for the magical night" scrawled on the back? Did they care that he liked green beans and hated brussel sprouts?

He smiled at the woman and nudged James's elbow—their long-established distress signal.

"Well, ladies." James clapped his hands and slid out of the booth. "It was great meeting you. Be sure to check out Kane's Web site for his upcoming appearances." Like the slick pro he was, James had the women shuffling away seconds later, content with their autographs.

"Let's get out of here," he said as he turned back to them.

Back at the hotel, Kane, James and Lexie met by mutual agreement in James's room. He and Kane popped a couple of beers, and James even convinced Lexie to have some wine he ordered from room service. They relaxed in the living area, watched ESPN and went over the weekend schedule.

"The car'll qualify well," Lexie said. "It's the same body and setup from last spring when Kane won."

"You know the drill, man," James said. "Stay patient and out of trouble."

Lexie nodded. "Be flexible early in the race, then you can bump people out of the way later."

Kane shook his head. "I'm not bumping anybody out of the way."

"If somebody's won't move, and you have a stronger car, you will."

"I don't need to win that way."

"You need to win any way you can."

James leaned back into the sofa cushions. "Kids, kids, let's not fight."

A cell phone rang, and James snatched his off the coffee table. After a quick grin, he rose. "I'd better take this in the other room."

Lexie watched him stroll into the bedroom and close the door. "The man has more women on his line than a fisherman has minnows."

"Hasn't he always?" Kane said, feeling nerves jump in his stomach again.

Why did being alone with Lexie always affect him this way? Why was he questioning the wisdom of his championship-winning crew chief and team owner? Why had they felt the need to bring *her* into the mix? They were doing just—

Okay, so maybe they weren't doing just fine.

He'd never made The Chase. His highest year-end finish was sixteen. He had brilliant people all around him, and yet something was wrong. The chemistry wasn't right.

But did he really need *her* to push him? Did he really need *her* to come along and mess with his concentration?

He'd been fighting memories of her, of them together, all season. He'd pretended his attraction to her had faded with time. How had it gotten so bad that he couldn't spend three minutes in her company without jealousy or desire— or both—attacking him?

They were inches apart. She sat at one end of the sofa; he sat in the middle. James's seat now seemed palpably vacant, as if his leaving had turned up tension that had been building for the past six months, and especially since yesterday afternoon.

If he leaned over, he could repeat the rash move he'd made on the plane. He could yank her against him. He could feel her soft, womanly curves pressed against him. Instead of that idea knocking him back to reality as it should have, every second that ticked past seemed encouraging.

She angled her body toward him. "You're no amateur yourself."

He clenched his hands into fists to keep from reaching for her. "Huh?"

"Fishing for minnows."

"Oh, yeah." The women in the restaurant. "Some fans are more enthusiastic than others. You should be used to that by now."

Eyeing him over the rim of her glass, she sipped her wine. "Funny, I'm not."

Her easy mood from dinner seemed to have vanished.

Her smile was tense. Her eyes glittered with…something the opposite of cheerfulness. Anger? Annoyance?

"It's weird, seeing you with other women," she added.

She'd always been amazingly direct—one of the reasons he'd first been attracted to her so many years ago. Was she annoyed the fans had interrupted dinner? Was she simply frustrated by racing stuff? Or was it possible his jealousy wasn't so one-sided?

Still not sure of her mood, he kept his tone casual. "After all this time?"

"Yeah. Though I'll be damned if I know why."

"Simple. You still want me."

She shook her head. "I can't."

So much for mutual jealousy. "Why not?"

"We work together, and the team needs us to be professional. You need to focus on driving. I have to keep everybody mindful of our goals. We have too many important races in front of us. We have a championship to win. We—"

He held up his hand to stop her. "I know."

There was so much at stake—millions of dollars, the respect of the team, not to mention their careers. If they got involved again, and it ended badly, they could jeopardize so many people's lives.

Her gaze connected with his, her green eyes shadowed. "So why does none of that matter?" she asked, her voice smoky and low. "Why, after Sunday, can't I stop thinking about you?"

CHAPTER THREE

HER CONFESSION still hanging in the air, Lexie watched Kane's eyes widen. He reached for her, then drew back, dropping his hand to his thigh. "I can't stop thinking about you, either."

More than anything, she wanted to lay her head against his shoulder, for him to stroke her hair and gather her close. She actually felt tears stinging her eyes for all the regrets she had when it came to Kane Jackson. "We can't do this. Not now."

"No, we can't." For a second, longing lit his eyes, then he looked down. "And I'm sorry about yesterday. When we…"

"Kissed."

"Right. *That.* I shouldn't have grabbed you."

"That's the most hot-blooded I've seen you in months." His gaze flew back to hers, and she smiled. "It was welcome in the professional sense."

"But not personally."

"We can't."

"You said that already."

She sighed. So much of her past was tied up in Kane. Those memories—of herself and Kane at seventeen, the realization that twelve years had passed, and she hadn't had a serious relationship since—made her much more emotional than normal.

After her mother's death when she was twelve, she and

her father had moved to Mooresville from California. They'd clung to each other, learned from each other and become friends far earlier than most young women did with their fathers.

Through grief, loneliness and adolescent confusion, they'd used racing to connect and fill the void in their lives.

She'd been comforted and exhilarated by the competition, by the sheer power and speed of those 700-plus horsepower engines, by the sounds of the screaming fans, by the new family she'd built.

But by the time she was a senior in high school, as she came to better understand her parents' great love for each other, and her relationship with Kane deepened, she realized she'd always be second in his life.

She'd dreamed of dating someone who didn't care about racing, or at least wasn't intimately involved with the sport. She wanted to talk about movies and music. She wanted to leave racing stats and strategy at the shop.

And that just wasn't possible with Kane.

He was a rising star. He came to life behind the wheel. In racing, he'd finally found a passion where he couldn't be compared to his father. And no one, not even her, could compete with that.

She covered Kane's hand with hers. He clutched her fingers. Her stomach tightened.

Longing, sharp and sweet, spread through her veins. So much time had passed since she'd felt such a sensation, she might not have recognized it with another man. But with Kane, the feeling was familiar, even if it had been years since they'd shared it.

"So much of what we want is hovering just beyond us," she said finally. "You want this championship. You *need* it."

"You want it, too."

"Yeah. I'd like to be the one to help you achieve your dreams. I want to see this team claim that trophy in New York in December."

"And we can't let anything personal get in the way."

She squeezed his hand again, then let go. Rising, she wandered to the windows and looked out at the downtown lights. "No, we can't."

"Why not?"

She'd asked herself the same question a million times over the last few days. She still didn't have a logical answer. Every time she put one and one in her calculator she came up with eighty-four. That seemed the number of people who would be directly affected by an unprofessional attraction to her driver. The indirect number was too scary to even contemplate. "Damned if I know." She glanced over her shoulder at him. "Though you were always a great kisser."

He set his beer bottle aside and stood. As he approached her, his blue eyes dark with intent, she tried to pretend she didn't want him to kiss her again.

Wrong man. Wrong time. Wrong place.

Still, her heartbeat tripled. Her mouth went dry. Even clad simply in jeans and a dark-blue polo, he managed to look sensational. His body was strong and lean from years of running and weight training. And though it had been years since she'd seen him without his clothes, her memory was really happy to fill in the details.

She fought a moan as he lifted his hand to stroke her cheek. His pine- and spice-infused scent washed over her just as his body heat warmed her. "I don't want to let this go," he said.

"Kane, please…"

He slid his arms around her waist and pulled her against him. "Please what?"

"We shouldn't—"

"Ah, we're making progress. Earlier, it was *we can't*."

She closed her eyes and indulged in a moment of stark hunger she had no business feeling. When had she become so perverse that she wanted the only man she couldn't have? What was wrong with a steady accountant? A charming stockbroker?

"You're so beautiful." He brushed his lips across her temple. "I haven't been able to stop staring at you all night."

Her pulse jumped. She wasn't beautiful. But somehow Kane made her believe it. No other man had ever made her melt so completely. By his touch. By the simple sound of his voice.

Why him? Why did it have to be him?

She glanced up at the hunger in his eyes. She knew what that look meant, what it could lead to. And it was a chance she simply couldn't take. One of them had to be strong, and clearly it was going to have to be her.

She forced herself to step out of his arms, then turned and ran from the room.

WEDNESDAY AFTERNOON, wandering through the race shop, Lexie checked the computer printouts from their earlier engine test on the transponder and was pleased with the numbers. This was definitely their number-one engine for the weekend.

That decision made, she needed to get moving to the airport for the team's flight to Bristol. She tried to tell herself she was just making sure every detail about the race car was checked, but deep down she knew she was just delaying the inevitable moment when she faced Kane again.

Early this morning she'd literally woken up in a breath-heaving sweat because of a dream about her driver. Added to that was yesterday's humiliating memory in Cincinnati when she'd run from Kane like a startled rabbit. Further breakdowns had to be mere moments away.

And she had a car and a team to get ready for one of the biggest races of the year—Saturday night in Bristol.

The half-mile track with thirty-six degrees of banking in the turns was the wildest, rowdiest race on the circuit. Tickets were nearly impossible to get for the fans—who numbered more than 160,000. TV commentators hyped rivalries. The drivers' tempers flared quickly and often. And the cars wound up bumping and banging their way to the finish.

Even with the pressure and craziness of her job, Lexie still looked forward to every race. She never lost her appreciation for the excitement or the drama. Something she and Kane shared. Something that bonded them.

She recalled the first NASCAR race Kane had ever seen. In high school, she and James had taken him to the track in Concord. Their seats were just at the exit of the pits, and she'd known the moment those engines roared that football's loss would be the stock car world's gain. Kane's eyes had lit like a Christmas tree as he watched those brightly colored cars with their intense, powerful engines roar through that first turn.

With pit passes her dad had given her, she'd taken Kane and James through the garage area. They met rookies and champions. They were embraced by the crews. No one asked about Kane's dad or James's college football recruiting status. No one knew who they were, and they loved it.

Through the rest of their high school years, the two of them bugged her for NASCAR tickets. Their love of the sport grew. They even built their first car together, which Kane raced, in secret, at the speedway in Myrtle Beach. After Kane quit football and James left Mooresville to claim his scholarship at Florida, they continued to build their racing team. Which, to some extent, had now become a reality.

How ironic that the sport she'd introduced Kane to had been their relationship's downfall. She couldn't deal with his fiery devotion to racing, his obsession to win, to prove himself to his father above all costs. Including her.

She got an engineering scholarship to Duke, which she accepted. She broke up with Kane and left Mooresville, promising herself that the next time she fell in love she'd find somebody who was stable and even-tempered. Somebody who didn't care if she knew a carburetor from a brake pad.

Somebody who wanted her above everything else.

Through her disappointment, anger and pain, she'd found strength within herself, and she'd sworn she'd never be second best again. The irony that she wanted him to be aggressive and obsessed about racing these days, when she'd so resented it during their dating years, wasn't lost on her.

"Have you seen Kane?"

Startled, Lexie glanced up at Kane's father. *Actually, I have, sir. See, I had this dream that we loved each other more than racing, and—*

"Lexie?"

She blinked away the remnants of the dream and tried to focus. "Oh, uh, he's probably at the airport."

"I need to talk to him."

"Try his cell."

"I already did. It's turned off."

With just about anybody else, Lexie would have offered a ride to the airport or at least further concern. But she and Anton Jackson had never gotten along. Kane's father had always resented her for introducing Kane to racing.

Which was fine by her. She resented him, as well—for years—because he thought she wasn't good enough for his son, but lately it was because of his lack of support for Kane's love of racing, as well as the change he'd brought about in Kane's personality.

At some point over the years, Kane's obsession with winning had been dampened by his need to get his father's approval. The fire of competitiveness she'd resented before—and desperately needed now—was diminished. Thanks to the man before her.

"Oh, well." She made an effort to smile at the man most American sports fans worshiped. "He'll be back late Saturday, early Sunday."

Frustration suffused Anton's sculpted features. "Is he really going to get into the top ten?"

"Yes."

"You're sure?"

"As sure as I can be."

"Everybody was confident before Sunday, too."

Growing more annoyed by the minute and wondering whether Anton was really concerned about Kane or just the questions he was bound to get in the booth during his NFL broadcasts, Lexie narrowed her eyes. "Mistakes happen."

"By you or Kane?"

"By the rookie who misjudged his passing distance."

"But if the car had been stronger, he wouldn't have been passed."

It was no wonder the man was one of her least favorite people. Hoping to simply escape before she said something she'd regret, she pushed for a wider smile. "You got me there."

"I want my son in The Chase."

As if his declaration would make it so. "Okay."

He turned away without further comment, though on his way out, he stopped to talk to the guys in the shop. He might be a jerk to her, but he did always make time for his fans. And she could be grateful that though Kane had inherited his intensity, competitiveness and charm from his father, he'd been spared the bulk of his arrogance. In fact, Kane's humility and down-to-earth nature was one of the primary reasons for his popularity with both fans and sponsors.

She, however, was completely immune to him.

Rolling her eyes at her delusion, she retreated to her office, where she gathered her laptop, printouts, cell phone and the bags she'd brought in that morning from her apartment. Bristol would be an important test for everyone. They had to finish well, and if she'd screwed up somehow…

She locked her office and vowed not to dwell on the what-ifs. She, her dad and the other team engineers had all consulted on the car's setup, as well as the strategy for the race. The team had run endless drills, hoping to shave even half a second off their time servicing the car. Kane had spent hours working out with his trainer and running computer simulation programs of the track. They were as well prepared as they possibly could be.

Still, it didn't seem like enough.

The thought of the upcoming racing weekend, plus

spending it with Kane made her stomach a bundle 'of nerves. But she smiled as she crossed the shop, waving to the guys who were already working on cars for the weeks after Bristol. She received several "good luck" shouts, plus a few good-natured jibes. At the door she wasn't surprised to see Kane's father still hanging around.

"Going to the airport?"

She nodded.

He graciously took her bags and carried them to her car. Okay, so Kane might have inherited a touch of courteousness from his father, too. "I'll follow you," he said.

As she drove her well-used Chevy Blazer, she put Anton Jackson—and the effect his appearance might have on Kane—out of her mind and recalled a night after a race in Myrtle Beach, when she and Kane had lain on an old blanket in the back of his pickup truck. Curled against his side, her head laying over his heart as he stroked her hair, he'd promised her that when he won the championship he'd buy her a pink Corvette. She'd laughed, then wrinkled her nose and declared when she drove a Corvette it would be red.

The laughter had died; the car and the championship never happened. She wondered if Kane thought about that night as much as she did.

She'd been hired to help the team, but she wondered if their past would make the climb to the top that much harder.

"YOU FEELIN' OKAY, Kane?"

Kane's eyes flew open at Harry's question. With his mind constantly on Lexie, he hadn't slept well all week and had apparently drifted off while waiting to board the company plane for the trip to Bristol. Risqué daydreams still filled his mind, forcing him to fight back a guilty flush as he faced her father, who'd slid into the passenger seat of his truck. "I'm fine. Just enjoying the last few minutes of silence."

Harry nodded. "It's an important weekend."

"Yes, sir."

An amiable man with a stocky frame and craggy face who managed his team through quiet reassurance, Harry lacked his daughter's temper and intensity. They made a good yin and yang match.

Kane was well aware of how lucky he was to have had Harry as his crew chief for the last three years. He was grateful Harry didn't resent him for the bad breakup with Lexie. Though he wasn't positive about Harry's feelings, since they'd never mentioned Lexie until she became car chief six months ago.

Given the building tension between him and Lexie for the past few months, and especially after their kiss last week, Kane had to fight the urge to squirm in Harry's presence. His crew chief would not approve of his driver getting involved with another member of the team. As a father, he'd probably be even less supportive.

"You and Lexie need to remember you're not the only members of this team."

Staring into Harry's direct gaze, Kane reminded himself Lexie had gotten her insight and quick mind from her father. "We do."

"You're both professionals, and I trust you to keep the team goals in mind."

"I am. I can handle it."

"Like you handled it before, when Lexie cried all the time and you stomped around like a wounded bear?"

She cried over me? was all Kane could think. He hadn't seen a single tear the night she'd dumped him. She'd just been angry. And resolute.

Harry seemed to read his mind. "Just because she did what she had to do didn't mean she didn't hurt."

He'd hurt, too. After she'd left for college, he'd raced harder, every chance he got. She probably thought his obsession with the track kept him too busy to grieve her loss. But he did that, too.

More deeply than even he would have thought.

"But that was a long time ago," Harry continued. "You've both moved on."

"Ah, yeah, sure."

Harry's eyes narrowed.

"We're allowed to have a personal life."

"Not with each other." He sighed. "It was Bob Hollister's idea to pull her away from R&D and put her on this team, not mine. I was worried how you two would work together again, but Lexie assured me you two were over and done." When Kane firmed his lips, Harry's tone hardened. "You've spent more than a decade trying to prove you belong in this sport. You've withstood the pointing and whispering, the doubt and the taunts. You're gonna tell me now you're willing to risk that for Lexie?"

Kane said nothing, though resentment simmered in his stomach.

"She won't love you for it," Harry continued. "If we don't make the top ten, you'll resent each other forever."

"We're going to make it."

"You're on the verge of showing your father he's not the only champion in your family."

Maybe, but no matter what he did he'd never measure

up to him. He wanted this championship for himself and his team. Not his father.

He was through listening to Harry. But part of him acknowledged he was right. Harry echoed his own conscience.

But Kane couldn't simply shove aside his attraction to Lexie. He was, however, frustrated and confused. After a long separation, they'd become friends again. They worked well together. They'd dated a mere three years, while being broken up for twelve.

They *should* have moved on. Until recently, he thought he had.

Now all he did was think about her and wonder what she was thinking in return. Memories of dates and conversations they'd had kept rolling through his mind. Regrets followed the memories. When would those thoughts spill over into their working relationship? Or, worse, affect the rest of the team?

He *should* suppress his feelings, but he wasn't sure how long he could. It seemed all he ever did was deny, smother or compromise.

And he was getting damn tired of it.

Kane shoved open the truck's door. "I'm done talking to you about this." He rounded the truck, yanking his bag from the back.

Harry grabbed his arm as he started to walk off. "Promise me you'll keep your distance."

Kane pulled back. "I can't." He stalked away, then paced beside the plane, pausing every few seconds to glare into the distance. Where the hell was everybody? The obscenely hot August sun beat down on his head, and he was ready to get on with this trip.

A few minutes later the team started arriving. Each man patted him on the shoulder as he boarded the plane, everyone looking somehow tense and hopeful at the same time. When James showed up, he tried to get Kane to sit down, but he refused, knowing he needed to face Lexie alone before they faced everyone else together.

If Harry had sensed something was going on, and James had already witnessed their kiss, then it certainly wouldn't be long before the rest of the team caught on. He wanted to warn her, to talk to her about the tension between them and see if that brilliant brain of hers could come up with a better solution than the ones he kept considering.

All of which involved inappropriate actions between driver and car chief.

What if they *did* give in to their attraction? Did he want to date her? Or was this a physical thing they could solve in one night?

Was it really possible to keep racing and their personal relationship separate? Brothers, fathers and son, uncles and nephews did it all the time in NASCAR, but then—

He stopped as he saw Lexie's Blazer pull into the parking lot, followed by his father's sleek, dark-gray Mercedes.

"Great." Just what he needed to add to his day. The legend.

He was inappropriately attracted to his car chief. His crew chief—her father—looked as if he'd rather find his shotgun than make pit stop calls. He had to face forty-two other drivers on the track at Bristol in three days. He had only two races left to make the top ten in NASCAR NEXTEL Cup Championship points.

And his own father had probably come to tell him about some new promo tour he should go on.

"Hey, Dad, Lexie," he said when they approached. His heart hammered as the coconut-scented lotion Lexie favored wafted toward him.

"I'm glad I caught you," his father said. "I need a moment."

Her overnight bag slung over her shoulder, Lexie avoided Kane's gaze and edged toward the plane stairs.

"Sure, Dad. In a minute. I need to talk to Lexie." He'd taken only a step toward her when his father grabbed his arm.

"She can wait."

Already annoyed and on edge, Kane glared over his shoulder at his father.

"You have hours on the flight to talk to her," his father continued impatiently.

As had become his custom, Kane swallowed his own needs and frustration and nodded. "Yes, sir." He didn't dare look over at Lexie—her stomping assent up the steps was enough indication of her mood. How many times had he put her aside for his father? For racing? For anything else that seemed important at the moment?

It was no wonder she'd wised up and dumped him.

"I'm getting a lot of questions about this top-ten business," his father said, his strong hand still clamped on Kane's shoulder.

Kane stared his father straight in the eye. There was always a measure of satisfaction in being able to meet him at equal height and breadth, especially after so many years of gazing up at him from a scrawny, weak body. "I'll get there, sir."

"You haven't made it yet."

"The team's really come together this year. We've got the right people in place. All three of the Hollister Racing teams are doing great. Bobby's in fifth and Richey's in sixteenth. Plus, we've all had some good tests in the past few weeks."

His father nodded. "I know you're doing your best. I'm just going to get quizzed about it in the broadcast booth this weekend."

You could show some faith in me. Shaking away the thought, Kane said, "We're doing fine. Lexie thinks we could win on Saturday."

"She seems sure of you."

Maybe it was the conversation he'd just had with Harry, but he thought he detected a sharpness to his father's voice. He certainly didn't want his father to jump on the anti-Kane-and-Lexie bandwagon. Being a man who'd married the sweet, manicured head cheerleader of his college team, he'd never understood Lexie's under-the-hood racing perspective, and he'd never been supportive of their relationship.

"That's her job," he said.

"And you're confident of her abilities?"

"More than anybody's." *Even mine.*

"I could help you find a new team anytime you wanted."

"Yes, sir, I know." The formal speech between them made him cringe, but they hadn't established a close, casual friendship like many of his friends now had in adulthood with their fathers. By contrast, he still felt fifteen—awkward and completely lacking in confidence. "I'm happy with the team I have."

His father slid his hands into his pants pockets and nodded. "Your mother wanted me to remind you to be careful. She tends to watch this race with her hands over her eyes, so be sure to call her right away if you're in a wreck."

"I will."

"Well…" He patted Kane's shoulder one last time. "Good luck, son. I'll be in Dallas to prepare for Sunday, but I'll get updates from my team."

He'd get reports from his *team.* His father's personal trainer, assistant and business manager all probably knew more about Kane's racing career than the man himself did. He forced a smile. "I'll be home on Sunday and actually get to watch the game this week."

"I'd go with the Cowboys." He turned away, then looked back. "If you ever get frustrated with racing, you know I can get you on with an NFL team. You'd be a great PR man, and they always need a sharp guy in sponsor relations."

"Thanks, Dad, but no. I'm staying in racing."

His father turned away again, heading toward his car. Kane watched him go, and a longing he hadn't felt in a long time washed over him.

His father had played his early career for the Dallas Cowboys, but had eventually been traded to Green Bay, then St. Louis. His mother had been raised in the Charlotte area, so that's where she and Kane had moved and stayed, while his father commuted during the season. Though the move to Mooresville was probably a move his father regretted in retrospect.

After his NFL retirement, his father had decided to focus on having his son follow in his footsteps. After that failed, he got a job as a broadcaster, where he was loved and adored just as much as he had been on the field.

Kane, meanwhile, fell short of expectations. He wasn't a big star in NASCAR. He was just getting paid to do what he loved.

On the topic of his father, his emotions were at war. He'd admired his father all his life. Even when work and other people got more attention, he'd never stopped being proud. He resented the standard of excellence his father held him to, even as he kept trying to reach those goals.

With a sigh, he turned toward the plane. He had a race

to get to. Maybe he'd never win his father's respect, but he had Lexie's and the team's.

Harry was right. He wasn't about to risk his career over an impulsive kiss and a few extra heartbeats when Lexie was around. That would be reckless, defiant and irresponsible. Traits he didn't have. Not anymore.

He boarded the plane, stored his bag in the overhead compartment, then dropped into the empty seat next to Lexie. She cast him a sidelong glare, fastened her seat belt at the pilot's direction, then stared out the window for takeoff.

What he wanted to talk to her about couldn't really be said in proximity to the rest of the team, so he put in his earphones and launched a heavy-metal song on his iPod. The drums and pounding bass blocked any thought deeper than what he was in the mood to eat for dinner.

A sharp elbow in his ribs jerked him from images of a two-inch sirloin. "What?" he asked, throwing a hostile look at Lexie.

She yanked the cord of his earphones, and when he clicked off the music, she muttered, "Between race engines and all that rackety music, it's a wonder you aren't deaf."

Since Lexie had zero taste in music—Barry Manilow being her favorite artist—Kane took that as a compliment. "Anytime you want to entertain me with something more stimulating I'm available."

"Dream on."

"I was trying to."

She rolled her eyes. "What did your dad want?"

"The usual—good luck, call your mom if you wreck."

"He didn't say anything about me?"

"Not really."

"Not really?"

"He wanted to make sure I was happy with you and the team."

"And are you?"

"You know I am. You and Harry are the best on the circuit."

"Maybe."

"You have two Cup championships."

She pressed her lips together. "My dad certainly does."

"You know perfectly well you did more work on Mark Clayton's championship than that idiot who was the car chief."

"Then why is his name on the trophy?"

"You want a trophy?"

Her eyes lit with frustration. "It sure as hell wouldn't hurt."

"No, I guess not." Harry's former car chief got the glory, and Lexie got a pat on the back. Still, there had to be some satisfaction in knowing you were a vital part of a championship, that you'd given a longtime veteran a dream-worthy farewell season.

By contrast, if Kane's career didn't improve, he might be out of a job before *longtime* arrived.

"What did you want to talk to me about earlier?"

"The usual stuff—the car setup, the schedule."

She shook her head. "You weren't trying to brush off your dad for the usual stuff."

Kane glanced across the aisle, where Pete and the jack man, Alex, were bent intently over a Game Boy. Their team was still a bit old school, as the two men traveled with him instead of flying in just for the race like the rest of the over-the-wall guys. But then, they both had other jobs—Pete helped James with PR on race weekends and Alex was the chief mechanic.

With those two occupied, Kane shifted his gaze back to Lexie. "How about another kiss?" he whispered.

Her eyes widened, then she darted a look over her shoulder as if checking for eavesdroppers. "You're crazy."

He trailed his fingers across her jean-clad thigh. "No doubt."

She brushed his hand aside. "Move back." Her voice, even in a whisper, was unusually high. "You've lost your mind. Somebody's going to see."

Didn't he agree exposing their attraction to the team was an extremely bad idea? Hadn't he just told himself he wasn't risking his career?

Yes, but there was nothing wrong with talking.

He angled his body toward her, blocking them to anybody's view. "I wanted to talk to you about Monday night."

"There's nothing to talk about. Nothing happened."

"Why did you run away?" He shook his head. "Not your usual fierce self."

"Can we do this later?"

"No. You'll find a way to avoid me later." He grinned. "I like that you can't escape."

Not looking at him, she gripped the armrests. "Why don't you go talk to James?"

Kane turned around in his seat. His best friend sat near the rear of the airplane, reclining and snoozing. "He's asleep," he told Lexie.

"What about Pete?"

"Video game." Inhaling, he leaned closer. "You smell fantastic. Kind of tropical. Do you still use that coconut lotion?"

She leaned down, putting her head between her knees.

"Are you sick?" he asked.

"No, I'm looking for my driver. Because you aren't him."

He patted her back, the warmth of her skin seeping into his palms, burning his fingers. "Sure I am, baby."

She jerked up. *"Baby?"* Rubbing her temples, her gaze darted around. "Stop it, Kane. You've gone too far."

"But I got your attention," he said against her ear. The desire for her, which had been humming through his blood for months, reminded him how good things had once been between them. "So that kiss meant nothing to you?"

Her eyes fluttered closed. Her face flushed.

"Ah, so how often do you think about it?" he asked, happy that he wasn't the only one with this particular problem.

"Once or twice."

"Liar."

She kept her gaze riveted on the back of the seat in front of her. "Wherever these feelings have come from, we're going to shove them back in the box."

"Can you do that, Lexie? Because I'm not sure I can."

CHAPTER FOUR

HEAT FROM KANE'S BODY rolled through Lexie. The temptation he presented was becoming physically painful to resist. Personal relationships for her were few and far between—and certainly none as potent as the one she'd shared with the man beside her. She wondered if any other man would ever measure up.

Maybe not. But she was determined to at least try.

She'd never be first with Kane, and she wanted to be for the next man she handed her heart over to. She *had* to be. And even if dodging Kane was slightly humiliating to her sense of personal strength, she was willing to sacrifice. Her body was weak, and her libido was deprived.

Some part of her had to handle self-preservation.

"I want to see you later," he whispered in her ear.

"I don't think that's a good idea."

"Just to talk. We need to figure out what we're going to do."

More talking? They were just talking now, and she was a wobbly mess.

"Come on, ba—"

"If you call me baby again, I'm going to clobber you with a carburetor."

"You didn't used to mind."

"I was seventeen and stupid."

He leaned back a bit. "There's an insult somewhere in that for me."

Since he'd given her some space, she could finally turn her head without fear of her face—her lips—touching him. She sent him her best haughty look. "You bet there is."

"You can't avoid me all night. We have a sponsor party to go to."

Frowning, she wished she could figure out a way to get out of that. They'd been invited to a cocktail-hour/dinner party held in the sponsor's luxury suite. She'd heard the owner offered lobster and caviar to his invited guests, so the party would no doubt be a major classy affair. "Oh, right."

"And don't even think about trying to get out of it."

Thankfully the pilot announced their approach to the airport before she could respond. Everyone who'd been distracted or asleep focused on getting their seat belts on and gear stowed before landing.

In the confusion of getting off the plane and transferred to the hotel—or the motor coach parked at the track in Kane's case—Lexie made sure she was in a separate car from him. And, with him ensconced at the track, she didn't have to deal with him being just a room or two away and popping in to talk about—or worse, pursue—this ill-timed chemistry between them.

She couldn't, however, stifle the urge to fuss with her hair and actually put on makeup instead of just swiping on a single coat of mascara later that night. However, the elegant, pale-green cocktail dress she'd ordered online—after James had declared her usual black pantsuit unacceptable—didn't fit just right. It bagged at the shoulders but was too tight in the waist.

Gazing in the mirror, she decided what seemed elegant on her computer screen looked like a mother-of-the-bride reject in person.

Plus, her makeup was too pale, giving her skin a sallow appearance. Her eyeliner was already smudged under her eyes. The lipstick felt gummy—it was probably old.

The new shoes she'd bought presented even more problems. First, she had to wind the straps around her ankle in some complicated twist that took her five tries to get right—those engineering classes clearly had no purpose in the real world of being a girl—then she had to hold out her arms to get her balance as she stood on the four-inch heels.

Not the kind of woman Kane was used to seeing on his arm, but would her future accounting, engineering or managerial husband be pleased? She hoped so, because she wasn't dressing up for Kane. Nope. No way. She was scouting for a man. A Sonomic Oil man. Even if he did work for a NASCAR-sponsored company, he had to do *something* besides obsess about engines, shocks, tire wear and lap times. He had to be somebody besides the man who'd broken her teenage heart.

When someone knocked on the door, she wobbled down the hall to answer. "I can't walk," she declared to James as she held on to the door frame to keep from falling over.

"You're beautiful," he said as he brushed his lips across her cheek. "Every man in the room will volunteer to carry you."

Feeling awkward, her face grew hot. Why couldn't she have fallen for James all those years ago? He and Kane were both charming and handsome, smart and fun. But, somehow, she and James had connected on a NASCAR fan level, and no chemistry beyond friendship had ever developed.

Her eyes—and her heart—had been all for Kane.

All the more reason to avoid him.

It took some skill and deception during the party, but she managed it—no easy feat in those impractical shoes. Not that she wasn't aware of every move he made, every person he talked to, every big-busted blonde who drooled over him. She'd counted every pinstripe on his navy suit before the cocktail hour was even over.

But tracking him was just habit. Right?

He looks fantastic. You so rarely get to see him dressed up.

She waved aside that opinion. Her only concern with Kane should be getting a fire lit under him, so they could get in the top ten.

She smiled outrageously at every accountant, manager and *normal,* upstanding type offered by Sonomic Oil. But, to be truthful, the pickings were slim. Most wanted to talk about Kane or her father, nobody was impressed with her ill-fitting green dress, others had had too much to drink and the rest had wives or girlfriends.

During dinner, she and Kane were mercifully kept apart. And the one moment when their gazes met, he smiled briefly at her, then turned his attention to the stunning redhead seated next to him.

Good. If he was occupied elsewhere, she could relax.

And that's what you want?

"Oh, shut up."

"Pardon me?" the chief financial officer of Sonomic Oil asked in a surprised tone.

Flushing at the idea that she'd spoken aloud to her conscience, she tried to put convincing interest in her tone. "I just meant 'you can't be serious.' You can't possibly have the capability to do a breakdown of the productivity of every employee every minute of the day?"

CFO-guy smiled. "Oh, yes, I do."

Okay. So maybe engines, shocks, tire wear and lap times weren't such horrible topics after all.

She moved through several circles of discussions, none more interesting or boring than the one before. She spent some moments gazing through the window at the brightly lit track so far below them. Thousands of fans would camp out on the grounds for the weekend. Motor homes and tents dotted every available square inch that wasn't already dedicated to track or grandstands. The infield was packed with team haulers.

She longed to escape to her hotel room, to rest and reflect on the upcoming weekend. Though the schedule was brutal at times, it kept her focused. It reminded her of success, not dreams unfulfilled. The extraneous stuff outside of racing was where she got lost. She didn't understand her place, or the rules, or where she might slide between the two.

"You look like you could use this."

She looked up at the dark-haired, dark-eyed, attractive man next to her and accepted a glass of champagne. "Oh, ah…thanks."

"You must be tired of all the schmoozing," he said, then flashed her a bright smile.

She sipped champagne and wondered when she could legitimately escape. "It's part of my job."

"I suppose it is these days. NASCAR's growth is phenomenal."

"Isn't it?" She never knew what to say at these things.

In the garage, among the sheet metal, engines and aerodynamic studies she was at home. Her feet felt firmly planted on the ground. Teetering on stilettos at a swanky cocktail party, however, she was completely out of her element.

Was the guy next to her resentful of their growth, was he on the "new NASCAR" bandwagon or was he somewhere in between?

"I had no idea," her companion added. "I grew up in New York. Now, I'm up to my ears in NASCAR licensing."

"And you like it?"

"Surprisingly, yes. I was expecting…" He shook his head. "Well, I'm not sure what. But aside from an accent or two, the guys and I are very much alike."

"And the women?"

He angled his head. "You're in the minority there, at least in the garage. But it certainly seems to be working. Bob Hollister tells me the team is on a roll."

"Bristol is one of Kane's strongest tracks."

"So I've heard." He flashed his smile again. "But I've also heard you're the strength behind the scenes."

Lexie finally realized this attractive man was flirting with her. Had it really been so long that she had a hard time recognizing such a phenomenon?

Yes, frankly, it has.

"I don't believe I got your name."

"Victor Sono," Joel, the team engineer, said as he approached, his hand outstretched. "His father owns Sonomic Oil."

Lexie vaguely recalled a son who lived up north, and she might have learned more about Victor if Joel's appearance hadn't been followed by Pete, then Alex. Pretty soon, she was surrounded by men. Not so uncommon given her job.

Tonight, though, these guys were looking at her. Not at her printouts or calculator or laptop screen, but her.

It was completely weird.

And undoubtedly the result of shock at their realizing she had legs, since her goofy dress couldn't be impressing anybody. She'd always been too much of a tomboy to have most guys take notice of her as a female. That was probably why Kane had knocked her so completely out with his interest.

She had to admit, though, that she was suddenly aware of her body, the swell of her breasts peeking above her dress's neckline, the curve of her waist. Feminine power wasn't a concept she'd ever embraced. She'd relied on her brain. But instead of scoffing at hair tossing and eyelash fluttering, she was actually considering doing such things.

Though doing it in front of her team was troubling. She needed them to move along. Victor Sono was a perfect man to spend time with. Handsome, intelligent, connected to racing, but not consumed by it. She wished they were in the shop, and she could send her guys off on some work-related mission.

Instead, front-tire-changer Pete was—if she wasn't mistaken—checking out her legs.

It was mortifying. Not to mention unprofessional.

When his gaze reached hers, she crossed her arms over her chest. "Can I help you with something?"

"You bet you—" He seemed to suddenly realize who he was ogling. "Oh, ah…no…boss. I'm, ah…good."

"I'm thrilled to hear it."

"You look really, ah…good." His face red, he nudged Alex. "Doesn't she?"

Alex's gaze drifted slowly over her body. "Mmm. Oh, yeah."

"Is it possible to have this be more flattering and less disturbing?" Lexie asked.

Pete shook his head. "I'm not sure, boss. I really didn't know you had legs."

"Not legs like that, anyway," Alex added.

"Personally," Victor broke in, "I don't know how you guys concentrate on your jobs with a car chief who looks like Lexie."

"They manage pretty well," Kane said, toasting the group with his beer bottle. "With me and her father around."

On a swiftly indrawn breath, Lexie literally took a step back. Kane's intensity overwhelmed her at times. His presence and his ability to command a room reminded her why he was good at not just the driving aspect of his job, but also the star-quality side.

A gift from his father, he'd probably say. A gift all his own, Lexie would counter.

His blue eyes burned briefly in her direction before his gaze swept the assembled group. "Right, guys?"

"Ah, yeah," Alex said, looking as though he'd rather be anywhere else. "Lexie is—" he glanced at her, then stared at the floor "—the best."

Everybody seemed to remember another urgent appointment about then. Within seconds, Lexie was left between Kane and Victor. The two men stared across her at each other, and while she'd sometimes had girlish daydreams about being fought over by two men—neither of whom could possibly resist her irresistible charms—the reality of being the center of a male stare-down made her hands sweat.

She sipped her champagne and tried to pretend she wasn't completely out of her element. "So…I assume we all know one another?"

Still glaring at each other, the men nodded. The silence lengthened.

"So, Victor," she began, "we were discussing the team. I think—"

Kane grabbed her hand and pulled her away.

Lexie dug in her—albeit shaky—heels. "Let go. Are you crazy? We were talking to him."

Kane continued to tug her along beside him. "You were talking. I wasn't."

Take-charge men were so sexy. Though her feminine heart fluttered, her practical side worried about offending their sponsor. What was Kane thinking? What was he *doing?*

She jerked her arm from his grasp when they reached the hallway outside the suite. "You're completely over the edge."

"You drove me there."

"Me? You're the driver in this deal."

He paced beside her. "Not tonight."

Sensing his mood was hovering somewhere between fury and craziness, Lexie fought to calm her racing heart. "Was it necessary to make a scene right in front of Victor Sono?"

"Yes."

"I don't see why."

He said nothing.

"You're just going to wind up having to apologize. And we all know how much you love to do that."

"I'm not apologizing."

Lexie's eyes widened. She wanted fire and determination. She wanted him to act more like himself and less like his father. But dragging her out of a party and insulting a sponsor was going too far.

"Why don't I walk you back to your motor coach?" she asked quietly and slowly. "You can get comfortable and relax."

"No."

"Do you want to go back to the party?"

"Hell, no."

"What the devil is wrong with you?"

He stopped pacing suddenly and leaned back against the wall. He closed his eyes. "What's happening to me?"

More concerned than angry now, she leaned next to him. "That's my question."

"I'm sorry about the *baby* thing earlier, when we were talking on the plane. I'm sorry for pulling you away from Victor. I *will* apologize."

"It's okay." She paused and drew a deep breath. "It's this thing between us, isn't it?"

"I think so."

"It's just the stress of racing," she said in an effort to convince herself as much as him. "Once we make The Chase, everything will go back to normal."

"What's normal for us?"

"Friends. Colleagues."

He lifted his head and stared down at her. "Is that all you've felt for me over the past six months?"

"It's all I *can* feel."

He shook his head. "That's not what I asked."

Warmth spread through her, followed quickly by guilt. This wasn't good. They needed their professionalism back, not more fuel for the flames of their attraction.

"So maybe we have some residual chemistry. It'll pass."

"When?"

"Eventually."

He slid his arms around her waist. "What if we get it out of our system?"

Her heart rate renewed its wild gallop. "How are we supposed to do that?"

"One night. You and me together. We'll get past this attraction, then we'll be okay again."

Oh, wow. Oh, no.

She braced her hands against his arms, trying to maintain some distance between them. "Won't work."

"How do you know?"

She was already struggling with distance from their past, and the last time they touched intimately was many years ago. As if it was just yesterday…

She shuddered at the very idea. "I just do. Besides, the risk is too great that it'll just make everything worse."

"Yeah, I guess it could."

"And when is this big event supposed to happen? We have a race to run in two days."

"Now's good for me."

Double *oh, wow.*

She wasn't tempted. She couldn't possibly be considering his rash, not-a-chance-in-hell-of-working plan. She stared up into his glittering blue eyes and knew she was fighting for her own piece of mind as well as team cohesiveness.

"Our romantic relationship is over."

His eyes flashed with old resentment, an anger she wasn't aware he still felt. "Not willing to give it another go? You walked away pretty easily before."

And it had nearly killed her. "No, I didn't, and you'd left me long before that."

"Just because I needed to focus on my racing didn't mean I didn't care about you."

"I needed more."

He sighed. "I'm lousy at relationships."

"Yes, you are."

"I wasn't suggesting we have a relationship."

She smiled weakly. "I suppose not." She patted his chest and stepped back. All of a sudden she felt overwhelmingly sad. "I'm heading back to the party."

He snagged her hand. "You could give us another chance."

His eyes actually pleaded with her. She was so startled she couldn't speak.

The only time she'd seen him even remotely affected as he was now was after he and his father had had a particularly disappointing argument over his football career.

"Just consider it," he added, laying his finger over her lips. "You don't have to answer now."

A *patient* Kane?

"I told you those anger management classes were a good thing."

A patient, amiable Kane on the track made her crazy, but what might those qualities do for him as a man? As his car chief, she couldn't encourage him to be anything less than singularly focused. And on racing, not romance.

"You hated those classes," she said in an effort to inject some levity into the moment.

"At the time." He shrugged. "But it worked."

"You need an edge to be a race car driver."

"I'm not a driver all the time."

If so, he was the first.

Music from the sky box floated toward them, and Kane pulled her close. "Ah, right on cue."

As he shuffled his feet to the beat of the music, Lexie moved reluctantly with him. Proximity to him in anything but a professional sense wasn't good for her peace of mind.

Still, she absorbed his heat and strength as conflicting feelings zoomed around her like bees. She wanted him, but couldn't have him. She liked that he'd developed a softer side, but his lack of intensity was affecting his driving, and the championship they all so desperately wanted. Pitting her personal needs against her professional ones was troubling and frustrating.

How would she resolve the two sides of herself? Was she really willing to risk one for the other?

She tried to push aside all that and focus on the moment. She let the music lull her, drift through the air and distract her mind. Even in her badly fitted dress, she felt pretty and feminine. It was such a contrast from her usual jeans and grease-splattered T-shirt. Many hopes, dreams and— frankly—fantasies involved Kane holding her as he was now. Focused totally on her. Touching her with cherished reverence. As if she was the center of his world.

Breathing in his familiar scent, she reminded herself their closeness would evaporate tomorrow. Or maybe even sooner. Their team was just yards away. They had an important race to concentrate on and couldn't dwell on their personal feelings. They couldn't afford to be soft.

But, oh, how she wanted to.

She indulgently, *briefly,* pretended they were ordinary people. They went to work each morning at eight, then clocked out at six, well, maybe seven. Everybody worked overtime these days, after all. She'd pack him a bag lunch, with a turkey on wheat sandwich, sour cream and onion potato chips and a vitamin water. He'd whine to his buddies about how she tried to make him eat better. She'd smile when he called her to razz her about it.

Once a month they'd meet friends for wings and beer, and twice a month they'd swing by the local Italian place for takeout and grab a movie rental from the Blockbuster next door. She'd cajole him into watching a chick flick, and he'd convince her to let him watch the last five minutes of ESPN *Sports Center*. She'd be an engineer for a car manufacturer, and he'd be a—

A…*what?*

A mechanic? A salesman? A forensic scientist?

Kane was a race car driver. Period.

"WE HAVEN'T DONE THIS in a long time, huh?" he said against her ear.

Her hips brushed his. "No."

Kane breathed in the coconut scent emanating from Lexie's skin. There were so many moments he cherished from their relationship—the races they'd seen together, the races they'd won together, even the races they'd lost together. But tonight none of that resonated with him.

He remembered the cards and notes of encouragement she gave him weekly, sometimes daily, in high school. He remembered the sighs of pleasure they'd shared. He remembered conversations and laughter. He appreciated her smile and her determination. He valued her brains and her body.

At the moment, it was her body calling to him.

The chemistry they shared—both on and off the track— was something he'd never had with anyone else. They understood each other. They *connected*.

The heat they created when they touched was amazing, comforting and frustrating at the same time. He'd never had that with anyone else. Still, he'd thrown it away. Lexie was right. He'd left them long before she'd stormed away from him that night in Richmond.

Maybe their relationship hadn't worked out before simply because they were young. Could this time be different? Were they crazy or brave enough to try?

As much as he'd matured and changed, he also knew there were pockets of anger and doubt inside him that he wasn't sure he'd ever resolve with himself, much less anyone else. He still had a lot to work on. He had to find a way to capture his fierceness for racing on weekends, and still be a normal person the rest of the week.

The career he'd chosen and fought for had greatly affected the most important relationships in his life—his father and Lexie. His racing had brought distance between him and the man whose respect and admiration he wanted above all others. His racing had brought him closer to the woman whose heart he'd once coveted, but it had ultimately driven her away.

Did he think he'd succeed today, where he'd failed before? They would both be risking a lot to find out.

At least they'd settled the past. He'd let go of his resentment for her leaving him and finally understood how much she deserved a man who could give her his whole heart.

Her hand curled around the back of his neck. He closed his eyes to concentrate on her touch, to absorb her softness, her cool breath brushing his throat.

Their chemistry was undeniable, but was she right, would one night together just make everything worse? Or would it open a whole new world for both of them?

"I have to go," she said quietly.

He clamped down on his urge to hold her to him. "I know."

CHAPTER FIVE

KANE FLIPPED the master switch, and his engine roared to life. The resounding echo from the crowd nearly drowned out the 700-plus horsepower rumble of the cars. His heart kicked him hard against his ribs. This race meant everything. His make-or-break moment.

After the week he'd had, he couldn't wait to get this race started. He was eager to prove himself. He was ready to focus on something he was good at, something he could control.

He had no doubt the night would be long and hard, trying his patience and the professionalism he was supposed to maintain. The heat and fumes were overwhelming. Turning the wheel so often, for all those laps, was exhausting.

At least he wouldn't have time to think about Lexie.

Naturally, that was the moment she chose to stick her head inside the race car. "Watch your fenders," she yelled.

In moments they'd communicate only by radio—but a transmission anyone at the track with a scanner and headset or any fan at home who cared to log on to the webcast could hear.

He simply nodded and didn't dare look at her. She was his car chief, not the elegant, soft woman he'd held in his arms a few nights ago. She was all business, and he had to be, too.

"Watch out for the rookies and the crazies. I heard Lomax and Devitt nearly came to blows earlier. Don't get caught up in that. Be patient, then make your moves near the end."

He nodded. His foot hovered over the gas pedal, and his gloved hands gripped the steering wheel.

"We need a win, Kane."

A military fly-over dominated the air. The crowd roared again, drowning his response of "I know."

"Be careful," she said, leaning closer and laying her hand over his.

Before he could turn to look at her, to see if he imagined the personal tone, the slight catch in her voice, she was gone.

Harry stood in her place. "Ready, sport?"

"Very."

"Keep your mind on the race."

And not my daughter was the unspoken warning. "I will."

"Clean stops all night. Clean and smooth. No mistakes."

"You got it."

Harry fastened the window net, then the car in front of him began to roll. Harry patted the hood, then stepped back. Kane followed the pace car and his three competitors as they exited pit road. They'd qualified fourth, and since starting up front, not getting lapped by the leader and staying out of trouble was advantageous, his position was ideal. He'd still encounter his share of bumping and banging, but he'd hopefully avoid too much craziness and desperation—which always seemed the hallmark of the middle-to-end pack of cars.

It was nearly impossible to keep the fenders pristine, but it was a matter of pride and survival that he stay as clean as possible.

As the field rolled around the track, he swerved back and forth, warming his tires. The day had been pretty hot, but the sun setting had cooled the track somewhat, and he hoped the change would translate to more grip for his tires. He mentally pictured the shifts he needed to make, and the way his car would look rolling smoothly around the track.

When the pace car turned off, the familiar rush of adrenaline would surge through his body. He couldn't imagine ever tiring of that sensation, that sense of anticipation.

The promise of victory and glory hung in the air for all of them. Every fan's driver held promise. The stories that would unfold had yet to reveal themselves. The tempers, heartaches, equipment failures and wrecks were only a vague mist in the future.

For now they were all champions. Each driver was equally certain he'd stand triumphant in Victory Lane. Each fan was sure he or she would be the one bragging to buddies later. Each crew chief, jack man and spotter was ready to be an integral part of both the struggle and celebration.

He and his team had worked hard over the last three days. He'd spent much of that time playing the video game version of Bristol, talking with the crew, performing the required schmoozing of VIPs, hanging out with the other drivers, and generally doing anything he could to put Lexie and the sparks between them out of his mind. He hadn't spoken to or looked at her in anything less than a professional way. She had treated him the same way.

And still he'd found himself losing focus at odd times. Not a good sign, considering his occupation. At the drivers' meeting earlier, he'd only half listened to the NASCAR competition director's warnings about penalties for aggressive driving. He'd stared into space and wondered how long he could keep up the pretense that everything was business as usual between him and Lexie.

"Got me, K?" his spotter asked.

"Yeah."

"A walk in the park, kid," Harry put in.

Kane smiled in spite of the nervous energy fluttering in his stomach. Time to put aside the personal stuff. Long past time. He had a job to do.

"I've got a feeling about this one," Lexie said.

Kane's heart jumped. So much for his focus.

Fasten your seat belts, guys. It's going to be a bumpy night.

Still, he liked hearing her voice in his ears, calm and reassuring when everything around him was about to go haywire. He didn't want to rely on her, but he knew he could.

"Go, go, go," his spotter shouted in his ear as the green flag dropped.

The field roared across the start/finish line and were into the first turn in seconds. The focus Kane had sought kicked in. As the cars scattered low and wide, all dreams of winning evaporated. Survival was the key. There wasn't time to concentrate on much else.

But if he could be consistent and get lucky…who knew?

He fell into a rhythm of acceleration, braking and turning, and was grateful nobody did anything crazy. Being Bristol, that lasted almost fourteen laps.

"Wreck in Turn Four," his spotter said. "Slow for the caution and stay low."

As he rolled by the accident, the safety crews were already out, clearing the debris and escorting the drivers to the waiting ambulances. The mandatory ride to the infield care center, however, wasn't going to be smooth, as both drivers were shouting at each other and punching their helmets into the air as if they'd like to do the same to each other.

Barely five minutes had passed in the race.

"Those two are going to be in trouble," Harry commented in his ear.

"I'm glad I don't have to face NASCAR," Kane said. NASCAR officials were serious about professional behavior on the track.

"Not yet, anyway," Lexie said dryly.

"My nose is clean," Kane said in mock defense.

He could practically see Lexie grin. "After only fourteen laps? Imagine that."

It felt good to banter with her again. Actually, it felt good to do anything with her other than endure forced smiles, awkward pauses and careful moments of avoidance. Maybe they could have a relationship by radio. But then there were physical parts of him that didn't see the advantage in that deal at all.

Since cautions always bred more cautions, it was a wild night. Kane stayed in the top ten for a long time. At least until lap 162, when Danny Lockwood tried to pass him, misjudged the distance and clipped his front fender. They both spun and recovered, but lost valuable track position.

During the caution, Kane fumed. His balance between patience and aggression tipped precariously. He'd never gotten along with Danny, probably because the guy was a reckless egomaniac whose uncompromising driving had already taken him out of one race that year. A few years ago, he and Lockwood had nearly come to blows after a race.

All year, Danny and Lexie had been cold to each other.

Kane had always assumed this was because Danny knew she was the best car chief out there, and his ego wanted her. But maybe there was more to it....

Lexie was pretty easygoing with the other drivers, crew chiefs and car chiefs. A lot of them treated her like a sister, and their respect was always present—either because of her father's experience or her own.

What was Lexie's problem with Danny? What was really going on?

Stay focused, pal. Race and deal with the rest later.

The anger and passion he continually fought against wouldn't be quiet, though. "That was Lockwood, right?"

"He's the only one in neon green I see," Harry said.

Lexie said nothing.

Which said volumes in his opinion.

His blood already pumping hard, the idea that Danny and Lexie shared some...*conflict* that he wasn't aware of made him want to punch the idiotic punk. He itched to talk to Lexie, to find out the real story.

Was he letting his imagination and frustration control him? Like Victor Sono the other night, was he actually *jealous* of Danny? Wasn't this what Harry feared, that a relationship between him and Lexie would make him lose focus?

LEXIE'S HEART POUNDED. The ground rumbled beneath her feet, absorbing the impact of the powerful engines as the cars rounded the track. She scanned the seemingly endless crowd above and around her, pleased when she spotted the pockets of yellow and red T-shirts and caps that signified Kane's fans. The rows and rows of stands seemed to extend so high above her, she was sure they reached heaven.

Maybe God will have mercy on us.

Thankfully, Kane said nothing more on the radio about Lockwood. The guy was a jerk, and she didn't want her driver's focus to waver. Dealing with him—and recalling the stories her father had told her concerning The Fight That Almost Happened—wasn't healthy for Kane's concentration and championship attempts.

She needed him to be a hell-on-fire driver and a patient-guy-who-understood-the-big-picture. Given all the shouting she'd done this season about him regaining his spark, that was going to be a real challenge.

Pacing beside the pit box, she tried to pretend she cared only about their finish as it related to the team standing. That was her job—get this operation into The Chase, then claw, implore, sail or luck their way into the championship. Nothing else could intrude. Nothing else mattered. Millions of dollars were on the line. Reputations and jobs hung in the balance.

They had a good chance tonight. They'd had good practices. They'd checked every screw and bolt. They'd gone over every procedure. The crew had marked each tire for easy identification and changing during the race.

"Trouble, Turn Two," their spotter, Bill, said on lap 232, his voice somehow calm and urgent at the same time. "Go high, Kane. Go high."

Lexie leaped onto the box in time to see Mike Streetson slide by, his car spinning. Though car and driver avoided the outside wall, the front end was smashed by another car. As Streetson limped to pit road, Lexie's gaze centered on her father.

"Two tires?" she said.

"No." Her father emphatically shook his head. "We'll need 'em all."

"But track position—"

"We'd still need another caution to make it work."

"Look how many we've had already!" Lexie said, leaning close to push her point. "We'll have another."

"It's a big gamble."

"It's not." She smiled. "I've got a feeling."

Her father rolled his eyes. "If I had a nickel…"

Into her mike, as Kane entered pit road, she said, "Let's go with two, guys. Two tires."

"Two?" Kane asked, doubt evident in his voice.

"Two," she said firmly.

He rolled in front of her seconds later, and she beat back the uncertainties that made her question her decision. The dance between logic and chance would always consume her job, but she felt confident with this one. She wasn't sure why. But when a gut feeling swelled so strong and sure, she was going with it.

She truly felt this was what made her both a good and unique car chief and engineer. She didn't just look at the facts and figures, she gave in to the emotion of the moment. A woman's instinct. She smiled inwardly at the ribbing the guys would give her if she ever voiced this theory.

As Kane rolled smoothly into the pit box, the crew jumped into their choreographed ballet of servicing the car. Lexie had seen her own team, plus many, many others, on tape and slow-motion replay. Old-school crews—without the benefit of helmets and fireproof uniforms—and present crews—with all the available technology modern, big-time NASCAR racing money could buy—still had the same job. *Get their driver out first.*

And their crew did.

As Kane roared away in front of the leaders, high-fives

and big smiles dominated the number fifty-three pit. Even her father, who was a card-carrying member of the Manly Stoic Club, managed a smile.

But within seconds, they were all shuffling their feet, sliding cautious glances her way then staring at the track.

Lexie didn't need a psychic to know what they were thinking: *Will the tires hold up? Did we just blow our chance at a top-ten finish with this gamble? We were running great. Did this chick screw us up?*

Maybe that last thought was a touch of paranoia. Her crew respected her, female or not. But in the closing laps at Bristol anybody had a right to panic.

She fell back on the old standard—pacing. She listened to the spotter's directions to Kane and tried to swallow the anxiety threatening to crawl up her throat. So much of racing was trial and error, instinct and experience.

Then there were the crap shoots. She'd taken one. She'd suffer the consequences or reap the rewards with the grace and class that was expected from the Mercer name.

But, damn, she wanted to win.

As she paced, as her stomach tightened and her anxiety ballooned, the crowd roared and pit road grew more tense.

No other caution materialized, but Kane hung on.

Determination, strategy or engineering made it happen. Or maybe it was all three, as her driver rolled across the finish line first.

Their team erupted with hugs, high-fives and, in her case, a few hastily wiped away tears.

They needed this not only for the points, but the psychological boost. They all had to believe they could make The Chase. If not, it wouldn't happen. The team had to believe again.

And tonight, as they rushed to Victory Lane in anticipation of meeting their car and driver, they did believe.

Teams graciously congratulated them as they made their
way to the spotlight. This was the part of NASCAR that
Lexie appreciated more than any other. They were all fierce
competitors, but at the end of the race, they equally understood how significant *any* win was.

In Victory Lane, Lexie embraced the jubilant crew. They
screamed and let the cheers of hundreds of thousands of
fans rain down on them from above. There wasn't anything
like a NASCAR NEXTEL Cup win—the exhilaration and
the relief, the sense that you earned the respect of your
competitors for at least that day, the wonder that you might
keep the job you loved so much a bit longer.

When Kane and his car rolled into their midst, she
caught a glimpse of his flushed face and wide, confident
smile. She knew her own expression mirrored his. She
would have loved to wrap her arms around his neck and
absorb his happiness. But their relationship was a complex
mix of friends, ex-lovers, professional acquaintances and
inappropriately attracted colleagues. And she honestly
couldn't envision anything else.

Confetti spurted all over the car and the crew. As the TV
crew zoomed in and the cameras flashed, she hung back
to watch James and her father approach Kane. She knew
they were handing him a bottle of Gatorade and making
sure his hat was on straight, the bill bent at just the right
rakish angle.

Like a flash from a movie she'd once seen but wished
she could set aside, she remembered Kane sliding out of
his race car after his first win at the track in Myrtle Beach.
Maybe a photographer had been there to capture the

moment, but they hadn't noticed. Kane's eyes had been only for her. He'd yanked her into his arms and kissed her long, slow and deep, much to the delight of the raucous Saturday-night crowd.

Crew chief and driver—a team and a partnership. Together forever.

But she also recalled coming to a race during college—after they'd broken up—as a pair of voluptuous blondes tucked their arms through his and kissed his cheeks. While she died inside and realized things weren't over between them, that things might never be over for her, he flashed the girls his mischievous grin.

They hadn't survived the stress and distractions. Together never again.

Where did this win stand professionally and emotionally? She didn't want to think about it. And though she was exhausted with the effort to balance the two, nothing could diminish the pride she felt at having her car in Victory Lane.

Through the swarm of people, she caught a glimpse of her father waving her toward the car. Her stomach fluttering, she quickly moved that way. Was something wrong? Why wasn't Kane getting out? The team, the media, the sponsor VIPs—every-freaking-body—was salivating for his big exit.

"He won't get out until you talk to him," her father said in her ear.

Oh, hell.

If it was possible to be annoyed and flattered at the same time, she was. Emotions she thought she'd buried over the past few days clawed their way to the surface. Her hands shook. Her knees threatened to collapse.

Still, she braced her hands against the window opening and leaned close to Kane.

His dazzling blue gaze met hers. Unspoken emotions passed between them that one day she knew they'd have to face. But for now things were simple. They'd won. And they'd done it together.

"Thanks," he said, flashing her a grin.

She squeezed his hand and felt a surge of desire, an electricity that never completely dissipated when they were together. "You were amazing."

He cupped her hand between both of his. "I need you, Lexie. And not just on the track."

She swallowed. "Everyone's waiting. We can talk about this later."

"Let them wait. This is my only chance to get you alone."

"Alone?" Though she didn't glance back, she could feel the tension, celebration and anticipation of dozens—millions if you counted the TV audience—pressing against her. "Hardly."

"But we could be."

Dear heaven, he was blackmailing her. He was holding people hostage in hopes of her compliance. And as much as she wanted to smirk and walk away, she instead wondered if she really meant that much to him.

She licked her lips. "One night?"

"Yep."

"I'll think about it." She pulled her hand from his, then backed away. Was she angered or flattered by his insistence?

Both. Which was certainly more complicated than one or the other.

A mass of jumbled nerves didn't help her make the most rational decision. Still, the timing for anything personal was wrong. The moment called for much more than just the feelings between her and Kane.

When he popped out of the car seconds later, the crew showered him with Gatorade and cheers. Jubilation infused the party. The eyes of everyone present lit like sparklers as they gazed up at their driver. They were all part of the team, but he was their symbol. Fair or not. Reality or not. All the celebrations and defeats rested on his shoulders.

Mere seconds had passed since the moment she'd held his hand, but Lexie retreated to the back of the pack, knowing he was a world away. He was a champion. A hero. She was instrumental in his win, but she wasn't with him. She probably never would be. And yet that didn't make the win less sweet.

As she wiped Gatorade from her stinging eyes, someone grabbed her elbow. She turned, expecting to find another crew member and instead encountered Danny Lockwood.

"Congrats," he said.

Having no idea why he'd thrust himself into their victory celebration, Lexie tensed. "Thanks."

"Personally, I wouldn't want a win at the expense of another driver."

"Happily, we don't have to worry about that."

"Yes, you do." A muscle along his jaw pulsed. "Your driver tried to put me into the wall."

"Not from where I was standing."

"That would be in the biased fifty-three pit."

"You're also standing in *our* Victory Lane." She smiled. "Do you need somebody to show you to your motor coach?"

"I'm not leaving."

She'd encountered angry drivers in her years on the circuit, but none of them had ever been so aggressive and disrespectful. And she'd had enough of this clown's whining. "Take your hands off me before I drop-kick your nearsighted, arrogant butt out of my victory party."

He angled his head. "Yeah, right."

"Seriously, buddy, you'll want to move along before somebody on my team notices you're in my personal space."

Almost before the words had left her mouth, James slid his hand around her waist. "Picture time. Let's do the hat dance."

During the dozens of photos, in which the team smiled beside the trophy, changing ball caps for every picture so they could feature a different sponsor's logo each time, Lexie put Lockwood out of her mind. Bristol brought out all kinds of aggression, and he'd obviously gotten caught up in the moment. She recalled tales her father had shared, how drivers saved their confrontations—and even the occasional fist fight—for a fast-food drive-through in Mooresville.

Right or wrong, the rumbles had settled everything privately, without a media play-by-play, without PR reps or commentary. It seemed nearly archaic these days, but Lexie liked the principle of facing your adversaries on neutral ground, of handling things honorably instead of throwing a national-TV tantrum.

But it was also a sport of people, not just machines, so the drama of life was emotional and often made public. Being a wildly competitive person herself, she'd never judged anybody who got caught up in the moment.

Unless they came at her, her team or her driver.

Small compared to everyone else in the garage, female like virtually *no one* else, she might be dismissed by some. But that was a mistaken assumption.

As Danny Lockwood found out rather quickly.

After the TV interviews, she, her father, Kane and James shuffled through the crowd toward the elevators that would take them to the media center. The only disadvantage to winning was that they couldn't rush to the airport and fly home immediately. There were media appearances to deal with first.

Hours later, when the press crush was over, she and James hustled Kane out the back door and headed across the near side pit road, then into the infield and past the rows of darkened, deserted garages. The rest of the team—and the company jet—was long gone. Her and James's luggage had been in the hauler, where it was being stored in anticipation of leaving that night, but one of the crew had e-mailed James on his BlackBerry during the media interviews that they'd transferred their luggage to Kane's motor coach. At least her shampoo and toothpaste weren't on a one-way trip headed south on I-77.

They'd probably wind up riding back in the motor coach. Maybe even driving it. She hadn't thought to ask James if Kane's home-away-from-home driver and unofficial team chef had gone back with everybody else on the company jet. Regardless, she, Kane and James were stuck together, bunking together—in a one-bedroom ninehundred-square-foot mobile apartment.

Oh, boy, that's *just what I need.*

They had gotten about halfway down the line of garages when Danny Lockwood appeared.

"Go away, Lockwood," James said as the rival driver fell into step beside them.

Lexie glanced up at Kane and watched his easy demeanor disappear from his body and face.

Not good.

She moved closer to him, hooking her arm through his. As if that would stop him from doing something crazy. Ha! It had been a long day. Obviously, she was delusional. And tired. And really not in the mood to deal with more driver drama. She wanted a nice, long, hot bath and a book.

Of course, Kane didn't even glance her way.

"Wanna tell me why you spun me out, Jackson?"

"That was your deal."

"Wrong, pal."

Kane ground to a halt and squared off with Lockwood. "I'm not your pal."

"You're not a driver, either, but that doesn't stop you from screwin' up the race for the rest of us."

Lexie exchanged a panicked look with James, who stepped between the men, while she tugged on Kane's arm. "Come on, guys. You wouldn't fight in front of a lady."

Lockwood smirked. "You're not a lady."

Even as Lexie flinched, red rage suffused Kane's face. And before either she or James could react, Kane had thrown his forearm against Lockwood's throat and pinned him to the garage wall.

CHAPTER SIX

"WRONG MOVE, PAL," Kane said through his teeth.

Fury coursed through his body. Sweat rolled down his back from the effort of not punching Lockwood's lights out.

"Kane, please let him go. Please don't do this here. And now."

Here and now seemed like the perfect time to Kane. He glared at Lockwood, who didn't look quite so cocky anymore.

"Apologize to Lexie." He said it slowly in case he was cutting off so much oxygen that the idiot's brain cells were starving. More than usual, anyway.

"I just meant she was part of the team," Lockwood gasped. "Like one of the guys."

Kane shook his head. "If you can't see she's a woman, then you need your eyes checked along with your ass kicked."

"I didn't mean anything by it, man. I swear."

"Kane, please," Lexie said urgently from behind him. "James, help me. What if somebody sees?"

Nobody was around at this time of night. It had to be after 1:00 a.m. Though that hardly mattered. Even if his father strolled by, he wasn't moving.

He was tired of being nice and polite. He was sick to death of taking crap from punks like Lockwood because the media or a sponsor or a fan might see, or, worse, be offended. He appreciated his fans and sponsors, and he loved his job. He was a professional, but he couldn't be a puppet. And while Lexie might think he was out of control with anger, he felt more in control at this moment than he had in a very long time.

"If you ever," he said to Lockwood, "look at Lexie again, much less say anything to her or about her, I'll finish this." He pushed back and walked away, leaving the other driver gasping for air.

Lexie and James caught up to him as he stalked farther down the row of garages.

"Nice work, buddy," James said with a grin.

"You two are crazy," Lexie said. "Do you know how much trouble—"

Kane laughed. "I thought you wanted me passionate."

"*On* the track! You can't go around—"

"Lexie, I'm really not in the mood for one of your speeches."

"Beer?" James asked.

"Beer."

Lexie said nothing more until they got to his motor coach and he and James had settled on the couch with a couple of cold beers, but he could hear her silent fuming as if she'd been yelling the entire time.

She stood in front of them with her hands planted on her hips. She looked so damn cute, he grabbed her hand and tugged her into his lap.

James raised his eyebrows but laughed.

"I was passionate on the track, you know," Kane said.

"I noticed," she said, squirming to try to escape his lap. "And if you don't mind my saying so, it worked. Sixth to first. I also never suggested you punch anybody. There's a fine line."

"Yeah, well, the rookie who spun me out last week just made a mistake."

"Whereas Lockwood was born a jerk," James added.

He and Kane clicked beer bottles.

"I'm outnumbered here," Lexie grumbled, finally stopping her squirming and crossing her arms over her chest. "And I'm really getting tired of it."

Kane patted her hip. "But we like having a little beauty and class on the team."

She glared at him. "I'm a professional, not a beauty."

"You're both."

"You're patronizing me. And changing the subject."

James ruffled her hair. "Not at all."

"Sweetie," Kane finished.

She caught him off guard by surging to her feet. "I'm taking a shower." She stormed down the hall, grabbing her overnight bag—which some thoughtful crew member must have dropped off—on the way.

"Your butt looks really cute in that uniform," Kane called after her.

"And I'm using up all the hot water," she called back.

"Should I come scrub your back?" Kane called.

"And I'm giving my *be a responsible driver* speech when I get out." She slammed the door.

"Drink up, buddy," Kane said, raising his bottle. "She's really worked up."

James leaned back into the corner of the sofa and eyed him shrewdly. "Do you really want to scrub her back?"

Kane took a sip of beer before answering. "Maybe."

"Hell, there isn't any *maybe* about it. Something's going on with you two."

Kane leaned forward, bracing his forearms on his knees. "Yeah. Yeah, I guess there is."

"Man, you know I think Lexie is the best, but you've got a banquet of chicks lined up. You really want to give that up?"

"I don't know." Though a banquet of women sounded much less appealing than getting Lexie to agree to their one night. After that night, he could consider variety again, but admitting that to James didn't hold a lot of appeal.

"It might be awkward for the team."

"So everybody keeps telling me."

"You've worked really hard to get to this point in your career. You need to think about that."

"I have been. It isn't helping."

James glanced toward the hall, then back to him. "What if you just…give it one night? Get it out of your system?"

"You're reading my mind, man."

"Lexie isn't goin' for it?"

"Nope."

James sighed. "Some win. We're supposed to be hoisting beers with the boys, not talking about relationships."

"No kidding."

James took a long pull of beer. "Forget Lexie. When we get back home we're going out. Just you and me. We'll hit the clubs in Charlotte and celebrate your win in style."

"Sounds great." He needed a distraction. Would a voluptuous female work where racing hadn't? Could it be that simple?

"It's just what you need."

Kane almost believed it.

When Lexie returned, freshly scrubbed, dressed in

cotton pj's with checkered flags all over them and smelling like coconuts—that damnable lotion again—Kane had to swallow hard and breathe carefully through his mouth.

Could another woman smell so tempting and fantastic? Could another woman—voluptuous, draped in sexy lingerie, less complicated, more amenable—really keep him from thinking about Lexie?

She didn't seem inclined toward speeches, either. In fact, she looked exhausted.

Kane rose. "James, why don't you use the shower next?"

"Sure."

As he left, Kane cupped Lexie's elbow and urged her to the sofa. "After we have showers, you can get in the bed and sleep."

Eyes soft, she lifted her gaze to his. "I'm fine on the sofa."

"You're sleeping in the bed." He avoided thinking—much less saying—*my* bed. "James and I can bunk out here."

"I couldn't—"

"My coach, my decision."

"Okay."

"You want some tea?"

She started to rise. "That would be—"

"I'll get it." Kane headed to the kitchen. He always kept a box of her favorite honey-vanilla tea in the cabinet, because he knew how it relaxed her after a long day and night in the garage. He retrieved a mug and brewed the tea, adding a bit of honey at the end.

When he handed her the cup, she said, "I should be taking care of you. You ran the race."

He smiled. "So did you."

As she tucked her legs beneath her and sipped the tea, Kane's mind flashed back to the raucous, confetti-strewn celebration in Victory Lane, then forward to tomorrow when James would make sure they were in a hot club surrounded by hot chicks and hot music.

All in all, he preferred this quiet moment with Lexie.

He dropped onto the sofa next to her. Close, but not close enough to touch. They didn't talk, but he was comforted by her presence and grateful he had her by his side—professionally, anyway. And personally, they were still friends.

But could that friendship survive the tension between them? Would the attraction fade and the friendship strengthen? Would taking their relationship beyond friendship destroy everything, or make them better than ever?

It certainly hadn't worked out the last time they'd tried. They were older now but were they wiser?

Lexie wanted—and certainly deserved—more than a guy who spent every moment of his life figuring out how to get his car across the finish line first. He wasn't sure if he was the man to give her that any more today than he had been twelve years ago. His offer of one night no doubt insulted her, not tempted her. He was thinking impulsively, selfishly, of his needs. Wasn't tamping down his rash impulses what the anger management classes had all been about? Wasn't that what his father preached continually? *Think before you act. The great ones are conscious of their image at all times.*

So why were his instincts screaming everything but restraint? Was passion a flaw or a strength?

When James returned a few moments later, Kane retreated to the back for a shower. The pulsing water felt good on his sore, tired body, but his mind was as cloudy as ever. He knew if Lexie so much as glanced at him in an interested way, he'd forget whatever he was doing, or toss out what he was "supposed to" do. He couldn't let go of the idea that giving in to their attraction would solve personal things—one way or the other. But would he lose his potentially championship-winning car chief in the process? And was it a good long-term solution for anybody?

You weren't ever thinking long-term anyway, right?

Right. Maybe that was the problem.

LEXIE LEANED next to her father under the hood of their race car for Saturday night. "I checked the spark plugs three times," she said, annoyed that he appeared to be doing so again.

"Doesn't hurt to check again."

At her father's calm response, Lexie stuffed her aggravation. She was tired and on edge. *Everybody* was tired and on edge. Except the unflappable Harry Mercer, of course. He'd been under the gun too long a time and too often to let a little thing like a NASCAR NEXTEL Championship get to him.

That was what the media said, anyway. Lexie knew better. She knew her father was worried and exhausted. He'd just learned how to hide it better than everybody else.

After making a delicious cholesterol cocktail of eggs, sausage, grits and hash browns, she, Kane and James had driven the motor coach home themselves on Sunday morning after winning Bristol. They'd sung goofy camp songs such as "100 Bottles of Beer on the Wall," then pulled the bus-chassis coach into the driveway at Kane's house on Lake Norman and proceeded to drink a few beers themselves. Just like old times.

August had come to a close. They'd raced in California and finished third. Richmond—the last race available for making the top ten in championship points—was four days away. They hung in limbo in eleventh place, with the twelfth- and thirteenth-place drivers only twenty and twenty-five points, respectively, behind them.

Bob Hollister had made it very clear at the team meeting yesterday that he wanted the fifty-three car in The Chase. If it didn't happen, he intended to make "some key staff changes." It wasn't just their ambitions or their pride on the line at Richmond. It was their jobs.

If that wasn't enough—and it seemed to her that it was— she was also on edge for another, far more personal reason. She happened to be walking through the lobby that morning when a stunning, buxom blonde had asked the receptionist for Kane. Since that happened several times per week, she'd initially dismissed the incident.

Unfortunately, she'd walked by the conference room at lunchtime, where the same blonde and Kane had been cozily enjoying pasta and salad.

Lexie's mood had gone south immediately afterward.

She *should* be happy. She and Kane had kept their distance over the past week and a half. They'd managed to work amicably. The Chase was within reach. Teamwork. Success. Peace.

He hadn't mentioned *them* again. He hadn't flirted with her, touched her or really looked at her. It was what she'd wanted and needed. It was what the team needed even more, though it was clear nobody but James had a clue how fortunate they all were.

Is he dating the blonde? Is he, even now, flirting with her, touching her?

The very idea made her blood boil hotter than brake fluid at Richmond. And how ridiculous was *that?*

"Something going on with you and Kane?" her father asked, jerking her from her thoughts.

"Going on?" she echoed stupidly.

Still tinkering under the hood, he said, "You act different."

"I do?"

"You've been tense. Jumpy."

Could she really fool her father? The man was more astute than Donald Trump in the middle of a real estate negotiation. "Nope. Not tense at all."

"Yes, you are."

"I'm ready for Richmond. I'm pumped and excited about The Chase."

"You're only tense when Kane is around."

"Am I?"

"Yes."

"Can't imagine why."

Her father straightened. He glanced around the race shop full of crew members—who were, thankfully, busy elsewhere—before directing his sharp, hazel gaze at hers. "I saw you through puberty, Lexie. Plus the first round with that boy. Now's not the time for round two."

Realizing there was no point in pretense, she sighed. "It's more complicated this time."

"You bet it is. Before, you guys were kids, goofing around, having fun winning races. You, outsmarting the other crew chiefs. Him, outdriving the field. James, drumming up a thousands bucks from the local Dairy Queen to buy equipment for the next race.

"*This* is different. The fans document every race-day call on their Web sites. The media discusses Kane's driving style, his mood and his image. Sonomic Oil gave Hollister Racing *fifteen million dollars* to sponsor this car. We can't make a mistake. You heard Bob yesterday. We *have* to make the top ten."

Her heart heavy, she nodded. "Yes, sir, I know."

She'd known all this before, of course. But having her dad lay it out so plainly was a painful reminder that her life wasn't just her own.

"Let's go outside," her father said, cupping his hand beneath her elbow, setting his wrench aside on the way.

They stopped on the octagonal-shaped wooden deck in back of the race shop where they sometimes had company picnics. Even though it was September, the air was still thick with summer humidity, the heat hanging on like a bad headache. She tried to envision the grass and the trees crystallized and frozen, as they would be when the season was over; when the championship trophy had been presented and the teams were anticipating the arrival of the holidays instead of another weekend on the road.

But she couldn't see anything beyond Saturday night. Make-or-break time. The knot in her stomach tightened.

"I know the pressure I put on you," her father said, leaning back against the deck railing. "I know how hard— how close to impossible—it is to have a personal life in this business. The pressure of winning and losing, the endless weeks on the road, the constant changes in rules, R&D advancements and team members all take their toll. Our jobs are all-consuming, and nobody outside our business can possibly relate."

"You and Mom did it."

"We were able to race as a family."

She crossed her arms over her chest. "It's lousy, you know. I can't date a colleague, but nobody who isn't a colleague will understand what I do."

"How about a nice accountant?"

She laughed. "You're reading my mind. Should I go for somebody at Hollister or one of the other teams?"

"Hollister, of course." He angled his head, his eyes bright. "Can't have you giving away all our secrets to the competition."

She'd needed this so much, to talk through the opposing feelings boiling inside her. How do parents know? "There's a problem with the accountant strategy, though." She licked her lips. "I like Kane."

Her father sighed. "Yeah, I was afraid of that." He shifted his gaze upward. "Your mother was the light of my life until you came along, then it was both of you. When she died part of that light dimmed. You're all I have now. All I want. The racing will come and go, but I want you to be happy. Racing makes you happy. He, so far, hasn't."

Well, if that wasn't it in a nutshell.

But Kane *had* made her happy. At times. In short bursts. Short, wonderful, *exhilarating* bursts.

Leaning next to her father, Lexie laid her hand over his. Her body warmed with his concern. Life hadn't always been easy for them, but they'd always felt blessed. They'd succeeded in the career they'd chosen, even though the one person they'd both wanted to witness their rise hadn't been there. Still, the racing had helped them focus and recover. A coping mechanism that had become a passion.

She couldn't imagine losing the love of her life so suddenly. She'd often hoped her father might find someone else to give the love he held in his heart. But he hadn't. Rose Mercer had been it for him. Now he had his daughter, his buddies and his racing. He couldn't seem to move beyond that.

Maybe that was why she sometimes found herself longing to find her own love. She knew how precious time was, how life could change in an instant. She wanted someone to share her dreams and joys, to hold on to through good times and bad.

"Kane doesn't treat you the way you should be treated," her father said. "I was devoted completely to your mother."

He brought me tea was all Lexie could think. Not much to most people, but she'd been immeasurably touched by the gesture.

Still, her father's words were true. Wasn't that the reason she'd broken up with him in the first place? She knew she wasn't the one for him, and she was tired of pretending to be satisfied with second place.

"I know," she said.

"You're attracted to each other, but does it really go beyond that?"

"I'm not sure, but the attraction is pretty strong."

"So I've noticed," he said dryly. "What else do you have in common? He likes being in the public eye. You hate it. He's a people pleaser, and you push people's buttons."

"He didn't used to be a pleaser."

"You're not going to change him."

"He's lost his fire, and it's going to cost him his job."

"And you can get it back?"

"Maybe. Bob Hollister certainly thinks so."

"I don't think Bob had in mind what Kane has in mind for recapturing his passion."

She glanced at her father out of the corner of her eye. They hadn't talked about her love life since she was seventeen—the first time around with Kane. "This is a strange conversation to be having with you."

"Who else are you going to talk to?"

Good point. The rest of the guys worked for her. And they were, well, *guys*. She had a few female friends, but they all thought Kane was dreamy and couldn't look at him objectively.

"So what do you suggest?" she asked.

"Don't repeat the mistakes of the past. And if you do decide to risk seeing him again, at least wait until the season is over."

"I can't put my life on hold during race season. We're only off for two months a year."

Her father snorted. "More like two weeks."

"Unless we get fired for not making The Chase."

"*Then* you could date Kane."

"If he treated me right."

"You deserve better from him."

Yes, she did. But there were some things she knew deep in her heart that were never going to change. "Racing will always be first."

"It has to be, when he's in the car."

"But isn't it first for all of us, all the time?"

"It shouldn't be."

She knew they weren't going to solve all these issues at the moment, but she felt surprisingly better. She hugged her father, realizing she'd be able to keep her focus the rest of the afternoon.

Even though it was only Tuesday, they had to have the car loaded that night. With a Saturday-night race, the schedule tightened even further. She still had to meet with the other engineers, and they had to double-check the templates, or else risk a possible violation from NASCAR officials when they arrived at the track for inspection. If they were off even a quarter of an inch in any one spot, they could blow everything.

"I'll see you later," she said, brushing her lips against his cheek. When she reached the door, she turned back. "You're not jealous of Kane, are you, Dad?"

"Of course I am."

Smiling, she walked back in the shop. At least she would always be one man's favorite.

For the remainder of the day, she focused on getting the car ready to be loaded in the hauler. Everybody shifted into high gear because nobody wanted to still be working at ten o'clock. Most of the team members had spouses and families to get home to, families the traveling team wouldn't see again until the early hours of Sunday morning. She was fortunate enough to have her family with her.

"You're coming with me tonight," a familiar voice said.

Crouched behind the car to measure the fender, Lexie groaned.

She glanced over at a pair of sky-high, hot-pink stilettos—one of which was tapping the garage floor impatiently. Her gaze slid up a pair of tanned, slender legs to a frilly short skirt, a form-fitting top, past a silky curtain of highlighted blond hair, then finally to the annoyed but lovely face of Hollister Racing's office manager and reception-area guard dog.

Her powers of concentration must have really kicked into gear in the past few hours, because it was only now that she noticed everybody had stopped working.

She rose and grabbed Cheryl Tolfort's arm, leading her across the garage, then down the hall to her office. As an afterthought, she went back to the garage and shouted, "Get back to work!"

Back in her office, she sent a mild glare Cheryl's way. Not that she noticed. She was flitting around the office like a cute pink bee.

Cheryl was fast.

Not in the old-fashioned sense of being loose or morally corrupt; she just moved quickly. She talked fast. She thought fast. She moved fast.

"I thought we'd agreed you wouldn't come to the garage on loading day," Lexie said.

Not abashed in the least, Cheryl waved her manicured hand. "This is an emergency."

Lexie instantly thought of—what else—the car. "NASCAR called. We're being fined for something."

"No, no."

Kane and James. She hadn't seen them all afternoon. "Somebody's hurt."

"No."

"Bob Hollister is firing everybody."

"Of course not. Good grief, you really do need this."

Realizing the emergency was anything but, Lexie moved to her desk, her mind already on the initial setup for qualifying. "Need what?"

"A night out with the girls."

"What girls?"

"Well, just me actually. I think you should start out slowly. Let me see your hands."

Before she could react, Cheryl had already snagged her hand and bent over it. She tsked. "Have you *ever* had a manicure?"

"I—"

"Is that really grease under your fingernails?"

"I'm sure it is, but I don't see why—"

"Do you even own a dress?" Cheryl's pitying gaze raked her body. "I'm not taking you anywhere in jeans and a T-shirt."

"I don't see what difference it makes since I'm not going—"

"Oh, yes, you are. Your father suggested, and I agree. You need to have some fun, take your mind off racing for once."

Lexie crossed her arms over her chest. "My father suggested?"

"Earlier today. Actually, I've wanted to take you out with me for a while, but I know how important this top-ten stuff is, so I've been holding back."

Holding back? The woman didn't know the meaning of the words.

"But since your father encouraged me, I'm ready to go. What time will all that junk be loaded?"

Despite her frustration at the ambush, Lexie nearly smiled. This was why Bob had hired her to run the front office. *Stuff* was the championship, worth more than five million dollars to the winning team. *Junk* was millions of dollars in cars, engines and vital equipment they needed to race in front of hundreds of thousands of fans.

Cheryl couldn't care less. She was unflappable in the midst of chaos and unimpressed by the high profile of everyone she worked for. She also wasn't googly-eyed with the drivers, other team owners or sponsors. She wasn't fooled by cute women who had an *appointment* to see Kane or any of the other Hollister drivers.

Racing, frankly, was way down her list of priorities. Lexie had to send her an e-mail after each race to let her know what had happened, so she could direct media inquiries for the next week.

"We're shooting for six," she said in response to Cheryl's question about loading, though she had no intention of leaving until much later. She only had an empty apartment to go home to, and she'd much rather work to keep her mind off Kane and his blond lunch companion or Richmond and its tire-shredding turns.

"Perfect," Cheryl said. "I'll make nail appointments for six-thirty. Tamera is almost always booked, but she'll make time for us. Then we'll—"

"I'm not getting my nails done. I'm working."

"After our nails are done, we'll move on to hair and makeup." She pulled off Lexie's cap and dusted her fingers over her hair. "Definitely a better cut, and highlights are a must."

Lexie crammed her hat back on her head. "I'm not—"

"*Then* we're going to dinner. Something light, I think. We don't want to be too full and feel logy. Then it's on to Neon."

Lexie was so startled she forgot to argue about going at all. "Neon, as in the Charlotte nightclub, Neon?"

"That's the one."

"I'm not driving into Charlotte tonight."

"Of course not, silly. I hired a limo."

"No. Absolutely not."

Cheryl ignored her and rolled on. "Clothes are going to be an issue, though. I guess we could swing by your house."

Lexie opened her mouth to argue, but Cheryl kept going. "But then again, a new outfit would be better. What size are you?"

"An eight."

Cheryl waved her hand. "Pish. You look more like a six to me—though who can tell in those baggy jeans. I'll call Alphonso at Nordstrom and have him pick something out."

Lexie sank into her desk chair. "This isn't happening."

"Yes, it is." Cheryl leaned over the desk. "And don't act like you're about to be tortured. You're going to be *pampered*. Every normal woman *likes* to be pampered."

"I'm not normal."

"You're telling me. It's four-thirty now, so I'll come back to get you at six, and we can get started."

"Cheryl, you're very sweet, really. But I don't have time for manicures and clubs. I have a race to prepare for."

"I thought you said the car would be loaded by six."

"Well, yeah, but—"

"And you are the *car* chief, right?"

"Well, yeah, but I have other—"

Cheryl dusted her hands together and headed toward the door. "Sounds like your job's done for the day." She waved as she walked out. "Six o'clock."

She was gone a full thirty seconds before realization set in. She'd actually agreed to a girls' night out with Cheryl. She didn't have time to play dress-up. What would Cheryl do if she simply sneaked out?

She could always take her laptop home and run through the computer simulations there. One of her engineers could finish up in the garage, and her Mr. Big Ideas Father could supervise the loading.

By the time Cheryl figured out she was gone…

The door cracked open, and Cheryl stuck her head inside. "And don't even think about sneaking off." She closed the door with a snap.

Well, hell.

CHAPTER SEVEN

THOUGH LEXIE PROTESTED at every drop of polish, highlighter and lip gloss, she was ignored.

Used to giving commands, she was rendered speechless several times when her orders not only weren't followed, but people talked over and around her as if she wasn't even there. Nobody would tell her what they were doing to her at any particular moment. And, worst of all, she wasn't allowed a mirror.

She could have pink hair with purple highlights for all she knew.

Or maybe, she wondered with a giggle—they'd plied her with champagne, too—she could have red hair with flaming yellow streaks. Then she'd match the stock car.

So maybe the coddling and attention hadn't been all bad. The hand massage was pretty nice, as was the warm, sweet-smelling cream they'd put on her face. And if she had pink hair, she could just stuff it up in her team cap. It's not as if anyone would notice.

Would Kane really halt in his tracks the way the guys in the garage did for Cheryl?

Nope. Not a chance.

"All done," her makeup consultant said, standing back to observe her.

Lexie's gaze flicked to the mirror, which was covered up with a big white sheet. She felt like one of the TV fashion victims just before their big "reveal." "Do I get to see now?"

"After you get dressed," Cheryl said, walking up with that stubborn look Lexie had gotten way too used to over the past few hours.

"How do I know my hair isn't pink?" she asked, rising reluctantly.

"Pull a strand over and look at it."

Pampering definitely made the brain fuzzy. She did as Cheryl suggested, then frowned. "It looks the same." Though maybe a bit lighter.

"It's not," Cheryl said as she led her to the dressing room. "Poncho off, dress on. We need to get going."

"What time is it?"

"Nearly ten."

"At *night?*"

Cheryl simply rolled her eyes and shut the door.

"I need to go to bed, not go out," Lexie shouted. "I have to qualify in less than two days, you know."

"Kane and the car have to qualify. You just have to squawk on the radio."

"I don't squawk!"

"Get dressed already."

Fine. One drink. She was having *one drink* at this club, then she was going home. They'd already done nails, hair, makeup and champagne. They'd even already had dinner, since Alphonso from Nordstrom had brought along Caesar salads when he delivered the dress—all part of the service, apparently, when you were a power shopper like Cheryl.

Lexie didn't even want to think about what all this was costing her. Cheryl had demanded her credit card early on, and she'd signed the receipts without even looking at the totals.

Hey, she could just bill her father for the whole thing. This was all his idea, after all.

With that cheerful thought spurring her, she slipped into the stylish little black dress—LBD according to Cheryl— and couldn't help but sigh as the silk lining caressed her body.

Okay, so the hand massage, the face stuff *and* the dress were all pretty cool.

Her thoughts flew back to the sponsor party at Bristol. The night she'd worn the ill-fitting green dress. Maybe she hadn't stopped Kane in his tracks, but the other men had certainly noticed her, even without the professional help Cheryl so obviously thought she needed.

She'd spent so much of her life focusing on using her brain power, she didn't put much stock in the fleeting thrill of appearances. But she couldn't deny how much she'd enjoyed throwing her team off balance and the flirty light in Victor Sono's eyes. There were men out there who'd appreciate her.

Why did she have to want the wrong one?

When she walked out of the dressing room, four pairs of eyes widened and four mouths fell open.

She lifted her hand self-consciously to her hair. "What?"

Her glam squad exchanged grins, then Cheryl grabbed her hand and led her to the back of the salon, where she faced a full-length mirror.

The woman staring back did not have pink hair. In fact, the color was largely unchanged except for a few subtle highlights. But the strands had been cut into a stylish, layered look that flattered her face much better than the walk-in cut she usually got at the shop next to her dry cleaner's.

The eye makeup and lipstick was also subtle and flattering, not the flashy, sparkling shades of pink Cheryl sported—which worked for her, but would make Lexie feel ridiculous.

The dress, however, had some va-va-voom, showing off her slight curves and toned legs. She resisted the urge to tug at the hem, but decided there was definitely something to leaving the dressing up to the professionals, instead of relying on her own, inept efforts.

"Much better than jeans and a T-shirt?"

"Or," Alphonso added, "one of those awful mechanic's jumpsuits. You don't really wear those, do you?"

Not often.

Unexpectedly, tears sprang to her eyes. Her job was to take care of the driver, the crew and the car, not take care of herself. She was touched that someone recognized her stress level had been too high. "You guys were really great. I know I was kind of a pain, but…thanks."

Cheryl hugged her. "You're welcome."

"Everybody needs a little pampering, doll," Alphonso said.

Relationships outside racing were rare for Lexie, and she promised herself she'd cultivate these new ones she'd made.

In the spirit of new friendships, she and Cheryl invited the stylists along to the club, where they were shown to a reserved, black-draped room with purple lights emanating from the ceiling that reminded her of a sultan's tent. As they sank into leather armchairs in metallic silver, blue and purple, Lexie bought the first round of drinks.

Their semiprivate room did nothing to discourage most of the male population from coming by to flirt with Cheryl. A few of them even focused on Lexie. She managed to forget about the race, the car setup and even Kane.

Until he called.

"Where are you?" he shouted over the blaring music.

"Neon," she shouted back.

"What the devil are you doing there?"

"Having fun." She thought she heard him cuss, but she couldn't be sure over the laughter, loud conversations and pounding bass surrounding her. "Did you need something?"

"No, not real—"

Cheryl snatched the phone from her grasp. "She'll have to call you back. She's busy." Then she flipped the phone closed. "You're off duty, remember?"

"But it was—"

"Even to Kane. In fact, *especially* to Kane."

Remembering her earlier conversation with her father, Lexie nodded. She was supposed to be directing her efforts at finding an accountant.

"You're right," she said to Cheryl.

"Sure I am."

"I'm entitled to my private time."

"Yes, you are."

Still, she cast a longing look at the phone lying on the small table between them.

"Don't even think about it," Cheryl said.

Lexie scooted her chair back a bit. It was sort of like detox, she supposed. She toasted Cheryl with her wineglass and firmly pushed Kane from her mind.

IT WAS THE SECOND TIME in as many weeks that Kane had found her surrounded by men. Not mechanics, drivers or engineers, but men interested in her legs, her smile and the sparkle in her eyes.

Even as his tongue threatened to flop on the floor, the

scene before him made him want to put his fist through the nearest wall.

He had no right to his jealousy, but that didn't stop him from selfishly wondering whether she'd even thought for a second about his "one-night" proposition. He at least deserved consideration, didn't he?

You had your chance, man. You blew it, remember?

And if he wanted another chance, it looked as though he'd have to wade through, then fight off, the grinning lechers surrounding her like sharks after a particularly luscious bit of bait.

She nearly dropped her wineglass when she saw him. *"Kane?"*

He forced a smile. "Mind if I join you?"

The four guys around her—plus a couple of the ones around Cheryl—all eyed him suspiciously.

Until one of them recognized him.

"Kane Jackson, the race car driver?"

Ah, just what I was counting on. "Yep."

"Hey, man, great race last week."

Kane rocked back on his heels and decided not to knock the guy's teeth out for staring at Lexie's cleavage. Just where she'd gotten that formfitting black dress, he had no idea, but he knew he wanted to rip it off her.

Slowly. And when they were very much alone.

He'd been offered a beer, met the astute style guy who'd decided to help Lexie show off her legs, signed several autographs and was halfway through a recitation of his win at Bristol when he felt hot breath on the back of his neck.

"Can I talk to you?" Lexie asked loudly.

He looked over his shoulder at her and—again—nearly swallowed his tongue. Why in the world was she determined to wear dresses all of a sudden? She was tempting enough in her baggy jeans and racing uniform.

And that was saying something, especially since he'd been presented with some equally impressive legs and cleavage earlier that day and hadn't been tempted in the least.

James wouldn't be happy to realize his ambush lunch date had done exactly the opposite of getting Lexie off his mind. Instead, he found himself comparing the other woman to his car chief.

Lexie won before the contest even got under way.

He couldn't see anybody but her. He didn't want anybody but her.

"Sure," he managed to say finally. He patted the arm of the blue metallic chair where he was sitting. If he could get her close enough, maybe his heart would jump back into his chest.

She pursed her lips. "Privately."

Though his pulse skipped a beat, he cast a quick, casual glance at the guys. He followed her out of the alcove and noted the hostile glare he got from Cheryl.

He realized he'd horned in on girls' night out, but he couldn't stay away after talking to Lexie on the phone. Neon was a notorious pickup spot—he should know; he'd picked up and been picked up there many times. Even beyond his own, selfish reasons for not wanting her at a bar like this, he didn't want her facing these guys alone. She was used to dealing with men professionally. She probably didn't even realize that most guys were not thinking about carburetors and aerodynamic packages when she was around. She was remarkably unaware of her feminine appeal.

And while he acknowledged he wanted her for himself, he could separate his needs as a man from his concern as a friend and team member. His gas-pedal-to-the-floor trip to the club stemmed from a need to protect her. Like a brother would.

Watching her cute butt sway ahead of him, he wiped sweat from his brow. Okay, maybe not like a brother. Like a friend. A close, concerned friend.

Liar.

Your blood isn't boiling over for your friend *Lexie.*

He wasn't walking close behind her, hoping to catch a waft of her perfume because he was worried about her as a friend.

It was Bristol all over again. Watching Victor Sono drool over her. Watching members of their crew stare at her with their mouths open.

And it wasn't as if his anger and jealousy at Bristol had been all bad. He'd channeled it into a win.

"Go home, Kane," she said when they reached the sidewalk in front of the club.

"No."

"This is *my* night out. You weren't invited."

"I don't think everybody else feels that way."

"You used those fans to get to me."

For the first time he realized she was angry. Really angry. And disappointed. "I was worried," he said, feeling his own temper rise. His intentions for coming to the club might not have been completely pure, but he also knew that she and Cheryl needed someone to look out for them.

She crossed her arms over her chest. "Oh, please."

"You're with Cheryl."

"So?"

"She's a man magnet."

"Oh, I get it. If it was just me—plain ol' dependable

Lexie out at a club, that would be no problem. But the hot-bod blonde attracts too much attention."

"That's not what I—"

"The guys aren't a problem for me. Nobody notices me, do they?"

"You're twisting—"

"Oh, but then I get noticed when people need tires or shocks or a wedge adjustment or their pistons rotated."

Pistons rotated?

She was really upset if she was rotating the wrong car parts. Each chassis, engine and roll bar was like her baby.

This wasn't coming out right. Yes, he'd thought she'd get more attention with Cheryl, but only because he'd pictured Lexie in jeans and a T-shirt—her uniform ninety-nine percent of the time. To him she was always stunning, but he considered himself a connoisseur of Lexie. No one saw her as he did. Other men didn't recognize her subtleties.

And he liked it that way.

He grabbed her hands and pulled her against him, then ducked around the corner of the building. The valets and arriving customers gave them curious looks.

She jerked her hands from his. "Go home."

He wanted to grow closer to Lexie, not further apart. For their roles as driver and car chief, communication was critical. For any personal relationship they might have, it was even more important. The problem was separating the two. Which relationship meant more to him? Which one couldn't he sacrifice? Did he want his Lexie as a car chief or as a woman?

He wanted both. But he wanted the woman more.

"Have dinner with me," he said, stepping close but not touching her.

"Dinner?" She angled her head. "We have the team dinner and RC car race Thursday night."

"Not with the team. Just us."

A yearning sparked in her eyes, then she dropped her gaze to the ground. "That's not a good idea."

He'd taken her for granted once, and she didn't trust him not to repeat that mistake. He'd played into her worries by resisting commitment beyond seduction. He'd planned to get her out of his system and move on.

What would happen if they actually had a serious relationship again? Was he simply afraid they'd fail? Or was he afraid he would never measure up to her standards?

And how would it affect the people in their lives? If they had a serious relationship, his father wouldn't be happy. Then what if it fell apart again? Harry wouldn't be happy.

What if they made themselves happy? What if he concentrated on her—instead of everybody else?

She wasn't a woman who slept with men indiscriminately, just for the hell of it. Like he would. His "one night" offer had been a cop-out. She possessed loyalty and subtlety and deep-seated love and passion. She didn't go for the moment; she held out for the future. For a man who would treasure her.

He desperately wanted to be that man. He just wasn't sure he could be.

But he knew one thing for certain. If he wanted Lexie, he had to be prepared to commit to her. He could no longer tell himself—or her—they were just going for physical indulgence, without all those messy emotions getting in the way.

Maybe he wouldn't measure up to Lexie's standards, the way he never had with his father. But he was through standing back and pretending she didn't matter to him.

Relationships were messy. Especially the ones that counted the most.

"I know I haven't been doing this right, but that's going to change." He drew a deep breath. "I'm not going to give up on us again. I know the timing's lousy, and I know your dad, my dad, the team and anybody else we asked would probably tell us to cool it. But I don't want to. I can't."

Her gaze softened as she met his. The struggle he felt was just as evident on her face. "I don't know, Kane. We're so close to the championship."

"It'll always be there." He reached for her hand, but she stepped back. "Have dinner with me."

"Like a date."

"Exactly like a date. I'll come to your door and pick you up and bring flowers." He gave her a mock leer. "I suggest you wear exactly what you have on."

She brushed her hand down the front of the dress. "You like it?"

"I do. But then, I always think you're beautiful."

"Since when?"

Ouch. Had he really been that lax with compliments? "Since always."

"You seem more into blondes these days."

He was going to shoot James. "James set up lunch with that woman. I didn't even know she was coming."

"You seemed happy enough she had, though."

Jealousy? He bit his tongue to keep from smiling. He was damn tired of being the only one turning green every five minutes. Somehow, though, he didn't think his happiness would go over well with Lexie. She looked as if she'd rather punch him than go out with him at the moment.

"I'm not interested in her," he said, leaning close. "I'm interested in you."

She drew in a swift breath. "I can't think with you standing so close." She tried to step back again, but she'd already retreated so far, she met the alleyway's brick wall.

While he knew he had to start thinking with his brain rather than more-southern regions, he had no intention of forgetting Lexie wanted him physically, even if her conscience was resisting. He had to work every advantage possible.

He leaned over her, bracing his arms on the wall on either side of her head but not touching her. Heat sprang to life between them. His heartbeat picked up speed.

Her eyes widened with alarm, plus a touch of desire. "What do you think you're doing?"

"Reminding you."

"Of what?"

"Good times we had. It wasn't all arguments and breakups."

She licked her lips, nervously it seemed. "I never said it was."

"Remember the races where we sneaked out behind the garage?"

"With James playing watchdog."

He still remembered the taste of her on his lips. She used to coat them in bubble-gum-flavored gloss, and he did his best to lick it off every chance he got.

"That was a long time ago," she said.

"We could make new memories."

"Maybe we could," she said slowly, her gaze searching his. "But not tonight. I was having fun."

The *until you showed up* was left mercifully unspoken.

"Let me go back—alone—and I'll think about dinner."

No way, was his first thought. Not back into the pool of smiling, flirting sharks. He tamped down the impulse to grab her and hold her against him where she belonged. She wasn't a vulnerable teenager anymore. She was a grown woman, one who'd tapped into her feminine power and wasn't about to let him call all the shots.

He had to learn to let her set the pace, learn to be a partner not a director. Or he was going to lose her again.

Like a gentleman from another age, he bowed. "As you wish, m'lady."

That, at least, earned him a grin. "I'll see you tomorrow," she said, ducking under his arm and scooting around him.

"Yes, you most definitely will."

CHAPTER EIGHT

"THANKS FOR COMING," Kane said as he slid his signed photo across the table toward a waiting fan.

"Good luck tomorrow night," the guy said, grinning proudly beneath his red and yellow Sonomic Oil ball cap.

Kane smiled back. "Thanks, man. We'll do our best."

Even though it was Friday night and the rest of the world was just now getting off work, the NASCAR world had been cranked up for the weekend since Wednesday when the garage had opened. Kane had practiced and qualified, then been sent to his sponsor's hospitality tent, where he'd answered questions, shaken the hands of executives and signed autographs.

Part of him would rather be relaxing in his motor coach or working on his plan to get Lexie to go out with him—she hadn't mentioned his dinner invitation since Tuesday night. But he never forgot the people who put him in a NASCAR NEXTEL Cup driver's seat. He never forgot who bought tickets to the races, or his hats, T-shirts and collectibles.

The fans bought his sponsors' products. They allowed him to do what he loved. They supported him—win or lose.

"Hi, who should I—" He stopped when he glanced up into the cleavage of a well-endowed fan. "Uh, make this out to," he finished lamely.

She leaned over, and he swallowed. They were in real danger of this family event becoming R-rated in just another inch or two.

"I'm Ashley," she said in a breathy voice.

Kane didn't ask her for the spelling. He needed to get her moving before the seams of her skin-tight tank top popped under the pressure.

"I think you're *amazing*," she continued.

"Oh, ah, thanks." He signed a photo, then handed it back with a vague smile. "Here you go."

She smiled slyly. "Anytime you want to party in Richmond, call me."

"Thanks again," he said, wondering if he'd have to hail down James for help.

Ashley-the-Buxom slid a card across the table. The sponsor rep assisting Kane immediately snapped it up. Obviously, James and his protective army of helpers had noticed something off about the exchange with this fan. "Thanks so much for coming," the sponsor rep said nicely but firmly.

As the next person in line came forward, Kane winked over his shoulder at his savior. With her brown hair, confident smile and professional navy suit jacket, she reminded him of Lexie.

But then, he hardly drew a breath these days without thinking of Lexie.

As usual, she'd ducked out of the sponsor function early. She was probably at the hotel, hovering over her laptop.

He also couldn't help thinking about Ashley—and women he'd known like her. There were times he and James had collected cards and phone numbers. Recently, even before he'd kissed Lexie and unbalanced his universe, the whole idea of women he didn't know who came on to him made him uncomfortable. What did these women really want from him? What did he want from them? Didn't he want more from his relationships?

Not that he didn't like to look at beautiful women, but some of them were just plain *scary*.

He guessed his feelings for Lexie were scary in their own way, but in a good way, like anticipating a wild race while he was running the pace laps. He might crash out, but there was a chance he might win the whole thing.

Thankfully, no more scary fans stopped by, and he concentrated on meeting his fans, taking pictures and seeing the wide variety of items they brought for him to autograph.

He was signing a collectible car when a chorus of murmurs rolled through the crowd. He heard a few gasps and a woman who asked in awe, *"Is it really him?"*

There were only a few drivers and people in the garage who warranted that kind of reaction, but he had no idea what any of them would be doing at his sponsor event.

The crowd in front of him parted, and his father stepped through the opening.

Wearing a light-blue polo, navy slacks, a dentist's dream of a smile and rock-star sunglasses, he still looked every inch the Super Bowl-winning quarterback. While many of his former teammates had taken to indulging in lush meals, spending weekends lounging at the beach house and occasionally playing golf, Anton Jackson still worked out five days a week and adhered to a strict low-fat, low-carb diet.

Kane felt a simultaneous pang of jealousy and burst of pride. Surely *some* of those superior genes had been passed on to him.

Since most everyone in the crowd was holding replica cars, hats or T-shirts with Kane's name and/or picture on them, the fans seemed stunned that a bigger fish had just flopped into their little pond.

"Quite a crowd, son," he said when he reached Kane.

Not sure of the motivation or purpose behind this surprise appearance, Kane rose slowly to his feet. "Yes, sir."

"Get Mr. Jackson a chair," he heard the woman who'd saved him earlier say from behind him.

James strode up and shook his father's hand. Notebooks, programs and scraps of paper were thrust at the legend as he moved around the table. People all over the tent craned their necks to stare at the commotion.

Kane stood in the middle with his heart pounding. Did anyone even realize he was still there?

He traveled back to the days when he was a kid, when women gave him fake smiles and men patted him on the head, all in an effort to get to the bigger, better man beside him.

I'm tired of being second best in your life, Lexie had said to him years ago when they broke up.

Her words were applicable to his relationship with his father. And they felt especially right at the moment.

He clenched his hands into fists and felt like an idiot for falling back into childhood insecurities and resentments he thought he'd buried long ago.

"I think you'd better scoot over," his father said to him with a grin.

"Sure," Kane said and moved his chair down the table to make room.

They signed side by side for a while before James announced that Kane had another commitment and needed to wrap things up.

Now that he really was exhausted, he was beyond grateful for his buddy's quick thinking, especially since he was pretty sure the only commitment he had was with a two-inch sirloin cooked on his motor coach grill while they watched that night's race on TV.

Amid waves and cheers, Kane, his dad and James jumped into Kane's golf cart and headed toward the drivers' compound. He'd planned on a relaxing dinner just hanging out with James, not entertaining his dad, and the closer he got to his rolling home-away-from-home, the more tense he became.

His dad didn't come to an event without a purpose—even if autographs and adulation were promised. After all, he got that everywhere he went, anyway. Kane had no idea when the true intentions would come out, but it had to be soon. His dad didn't like wasting time. And Kane sincerely doubted he'd put in an appearance just to demonstrate his support.

But, to be fair, he also didn't purposely intend to over-shadow his son. He hadn't come to the hospitality tent to be the star. He just always was. The spotlight was as intimate a part of him as his skin.

When they stepped inside, Kane looked around as if seeing his surroundings for the first time. Sometimes his fortune washed over him, taking him back to his first year on the Cup circuit five years ago, when he'd walked into his brand-new motor coach as a rookie, amazed at the level he'd risen to, awed by the influence he now possessed. He'd wanted a place to relax and hang out with his friends and teammates. Nothing too garish or overly commercial. No sponsor logos on the floor mats or oil-can-shaped faucets. He loved the beach—the Hollisters owned a house in Kauai they offered to him on the rare break from the track—and he didn't want lots of stripes or flowers. He'd given these directions to the decorator, and she'd created an amazing retreat.

She'd decked out the furniture in neutral colors with a slight Asian influence—bamboo shades and place mats and simple, black-framed prints of his racing wins. His bedroom sported several shades of blue and reminded him of the ocean, plus it was a nice contrast to the red and yellow uniforms he wore all the time.

"How about a beer?" his dad asked, dropping onto the sofa.

"Sure," Kane said as he headed to the fridge. He could use one himself.

James got his own beer, then slid outside to fire up the grill. Kane carried his bottle and one for his dad over to the sofa. "What's up?"

His dad smiled. "Up?"

"With this surprise visit." He settled onto the other end of the sofa. "Is anything wrong?"

"Can't I show support for my son?"

"Sure." *You just don't do it that often.*

"I wanted to cheer you on. It's a big weekend."

"Yeah, it is." *And the Cowboys have Sunday off, so he doesn't have a broadcast to do.* "You're staying for the race?"

He nodded and sipped his beer. "I even convinced your mother to come up tomorrow afternoon."

Kane raised his eyebrows and hoped his dad had the sense to find her a luxury suite to relax in. The temperature was supposed to be in the high eighties at race time. His mom was a delicate Southern lady who considered sweating only half a step above mud wrestling.

"You know she doesn't like the noise and crowds, but she realizes how important this race is to you."

"Mmm."

"Why are you staring at me like I've grown two heads? I had the weekend off and decided to spend it with my son. I know you've been under a lot of pressure lately, and I wanted you to realize I'm behind you. I surprised you because I had a previous commitment that I've been trying to get out of for weeks. I didn't want to tell you I would come, then disappoint you. Would you rather I leave?"

Embarrassed by his suspicion, Kane shook his head. His dad had never been enthusiastic about his driving, but he'd followed his career closely and always assured him he had other options if racing ever lost its allure. Kane had usually taken that as criticism, but many drivers only knew racing. If their career bit the dust, they had nothing else. Thanks to his dad's talent and sacrifices, Kane had enjoyed a privileged childhood and the freedom to pursue whatever dreams he chose.

Even a few weeks ago when his dad had questioned whether the team could get in the top ten, he'd offered to find Kane a better team. Instead of being critical, maybe he'd been trying to help, to let him know he deserved the best.

Kane stared at the floor. "Sorry, Dad, I'm just on edge."

His dad patted his leg. "Easy to understand. Everything's on the line tomorrow night."

Knowing he was one of the few people who could relate to the pressure, Kane nodded. "Thanks for coming. It means a lot."

The door swung open, and James walked inside. He took in the scene quickly. "How much male bonding do we actually have to do? I'm starving."

As they laughed, the tension fled. James always had that effect on people. He knew how to read a room of sponsors, drivers or mechanics. He also knew how to read a woman and a balance sheet. He was the only person Kane trusted unconditionally.

The three of them had a great time watching the NASCAR Busch Series race and sharing old football stories during commercials. The night reminded Kane how great a storyteller his dad was. He wasn't a has-been-wishing-for-the-good-ol'-days guy. He talked about the past with a been-there-done-that nonchalance and humility that never failed to impress his audience.

Including his son.

After football, they even discussed tomorrow's race when his dad asked him about strategy and goals. He wanted to understand the track and the importance of breaks, why the turns were so difficult and the allure of night racing.

It was the longest Kane could ever remember talking to his dad about racing in one sitting. And without judgments or skepticism about the operation or his decisions.

Even after his dad left for his hotel, Kane and James talked about his sudden interest in their sport.

"Man, that was just plain weird," James said as he closed the door behind Kane's dad.

"You're not kidding."

"The Cowboys are off this weekend?"

"Yep."

"There's no doubt the man can read a defensive line and pick out penalties for the TV audience, but interest in tire compounds and brake rotors? What's up with that?"

"I have no idea."

James turned his head briefly toward the TV, where a reporter was interviewing the race winner, then he sat on the sofa. "You think he's finally coming around?"

"Still have no idea."

Kane was optimistic and skeptical. Was that even possible? He needed some sleep. Maybe he was getting punchy from the pressure.

"Fans loved him at the autograph session," James commented.

"Don't they always?"

Kane flipped channels. The baseball playoffs were boring, so he focused on the college football polls. Florida was doing well, so James would be happy. Maybe they could invite a few of the alumni players up for a race if they made the top ten. Well, definitely they could if they didn't make it, since life as they all knew it would come to a sudden, grinding halt. Given this week's warning by Bob Hollister, some of them—especially Kane—might be out of a job.

"I think he's up to something," James said, though he was slumped in the recliner and didn't look like he was planning to pursue the topic too strongly.

"Maybe, but what?"

"Publicity for him when you make the top ten?"

"What does he need my publicity for? Half the people he knows don't even consider what I do a sport."

"True."

He wanted to find something to be aggravated about with his dad's visit, but either nothing was there or he was too tired and too full to care. "The hell with it."

"You always have me," James said.

Kane glanced over at him. With both his professional and personal lives converging and chaotic, friends like James were so important. "Thanks, buddy."

"At least until a really big-busted blonde comes along."

THE NEXT MORNING Lexie paused before she knocked on the door of Kane's motor coach. The newspaper she clutched in her hands was damp with sweat. The knot in the pit of her stomach tightened. Happy Hour practice was still a couple of hours away, and Kane wasn't his best in the morning, but she knew he'd want to see the article.

Well, he wouldn't *want* to see it, but he had to. And it was up to her to be the bearer of lousy news.

She had diagnostics to run, parts to go over, operations to review, a team to lead and last-minute orders from her father to follow. But this morning she was Messenger Girl.

Ah, the luxurious life of a NASCAR car chief.

She opened the paper and glanced down at the front page of the sports section of the *Richmond Times-Dispatch*.

While other NFL greats are starting their own team, Anton Jackson probably doesn't even know his way to the garage.

The Hall of Fame quarterback and broadcaster has never been a vocal supporter of his son's NASCAR dreams—a fact made all too evident by his continued absence at racing events. A source close to the team admits their driver doesn't have a close relationship with his father.

"We never see him," the source says. "It's an embarrassment."

Lexie cringed again. She'd never been much of an Anton Jackson fan, but the article was just plain mean. She had no idea who the "source close to the team" was, but from long experience she recognized it could be anybody from a member of another team who happened to walk by their garage to Bob Hollister himself.

Bottom line?

They didn't need this. Not now.

But they would have to deal with it. Now.

The media—both print and visual—was just yards away. There was no way the journalists could pass up the chance to question Kane about the hot-button father issue. Their distance had been a whispered thing in the garage for years, and most people had dismissed it as gossip, but now it was out there. Part truth, part sensationalism.

And *out there*.

Before she could knock, the door cracked, and James's head appeared around the corner. "Did you want to come in, or just hang out there?"

She was so glad to see James, she nearly cried. Though he stayed in a hotel on race weekends, he sometimes crashed on Kane's sofa if they had stayed up late the night before playing video games.

"Is Kane up?"

"That's rhetorical, right?"

That meant no. Just as well. She could use a cup of coffee to fortify her. And maybe a shot of whiskey. And maybe some cucumbers over her eyes and soft music playing in the background—hey, she'd learned a lot during that makeover Cheryl had forced her into.

Once she'd settled at the bar with a mug of James's famous French-roast coffee, he nodded at the white elephant in the room—the newspaper she'd laid beside her. "Anything interesting this morning?"

"Yep."

"Good?"

"Nope."

"Bad?"

"Yep."

"Gee golly, Betty-Sue, did the Russians drop the bomb?"

"Somebody did."

"You know you're making me crazy."

Lexie blew on the surface of her coffee, then sipped. "Yep."

"Give me the damn thing."

She handed it over without comment and continued to sip as he read. The warmth that spread through her body wasn't just because of the coffee. She now had an ally for facing Kane. It would still be bad, but she wouldn't be alone, and with James's help, maybe they could come up with a response before the rest of the NASCAR world even rolled out of bed.

"Hell," James said, setting down his mug.

"Yep."

"Who's the 'source close to the team'?"

"Got me. Have you given any quotes to Terry A. Lufton lately?"

"Humor? You think you're funny this early in the morning?"

"It's gotta be better than crying or screaming."

James dropped the newspaper on the bar. "This isn't good."

"Nope."

"He was here."

She looked over at him. "I hope he's still here. We have practice."

"Not Kane. I meant Mr. Football. He was here last night."

"Kane's father was here?"

James took a deep gulp of coffee. "He showed up at the hospitality tent last night. He and Kane signed autographs for a while, then he came back here with us and had dinner. We wondered what was up." He paused and met her gaze. His eyes were no longer bright and teasing. "I guess we know what it was about now."

"I guess so."

Lexie hadn't come close to anticipating this turn of events. The article was accurate in saying that Kane's father probably couldn't find his way to the garage. He hardly *ever* came to races. But she considered the details of their relationship private. Plus, Kane had enough to worry about without adding family drama.

Still, she wondered about Kane's dad. Had he been tipped off to the release of the article? And, if so, was he *that* concerned about PR? Did it really take negative publicity to bring him to his son's side when he needed him?

She didn't want to answer any of the questions zooming around her head. Neither, she assumed, did James. "Is there any liquor in this joint?"

"It's seven-thirty in the morning."

"You got a better idea?"

"No."

Still, they didn't go on a search for booze. They groused into their coffee and played poker to determine who had to break the news. By the time Kane shuffled into the room, their tension had reached ridiculous proportions.

Kane walked by them, poured himself a cup of coffee, then watched them over the rim of the mug. "What's up?"

Rendered embarrassingly speechless by the sight of

Kane strolling by, exposing his abs and shoulders by wearing nothing but a pair of sweatpants barely hanging on to his hips, Lexie simply stared at him.

With a long-suffering sigh, James laid the newspaper on the bar. "Something you need to read, buddy."

Men! He couldn't just spring it on him like that. She reached for the paper, but Kane had gotten there first. Her hand wound up covering his. He stilled and glanced at her.

"Problem?" he asked, his blue eyes sharp and focused despite the early hour.

Heat radiated up her arm. In fact, she wouldn't have been surprised to see smoke emanate from her fingertips. Why did he always manage to affect her this way?

Just like the other night at the club, when she'd been so determined to cast him as the fun-spoiler bad guy, he'd bowed like freakin' Rhett Butler and left the party he'd been so determined to disrupt. His passion and focus on the track at Bristol had been amazing, exactly what she'd been pushing for all season. His passion and focus with her had her thoughts scattering and her practical side desperately searching for a reason to find fault with him, so she could protect her heart.

If only his body wasn't such a distraction…

She jerked her attention back to her poker hand. "I, uh, does a flush beat a straight or the other way around?"

James tossed his cards on the bar. "Oh, please, woman."

She glared at him. *"Woman?"*

Fueling her anger and frustration was the sudden recollection that James had been the one who'd invited the curvy blonde to lunch. Hoping to distract his buddy from her, no doubt. The traitor. "Listen, PR Boy, I've had about enough of you and your—"

"Time out, guys," Kane said, grasping the newspaper from beneath Lexie's hand at the same time. "How bad can it be?"

"It's—"

James kicked her lightly and shook his head. "Just read it," he said to Kane.

While Kane read silently, Lexie glanced at James's cards, which lay faceup on the bar. "I had a straight, by the way," she whispered, laying her cards out in a fan. "That beats your two pair without even breathing hard."

"What's with you?" he said in a low voice while Kane read.

She pressed her lips together. "I'm just thinking I could use a blond lunch date."

"I was trying to help," James had the nerve to whisper back.

"Stop. Immediately."

"You want me to set you up with a blonde, too?"

"No. I can handle my own social life, thank you."

"What social life?"

Their whispered argument was interrupted by Kane tossing the newspaper on the bar. "I guess we know why Dad was here last night."

"Maybe not," Lexie said. "He may not even know about the article."

"I'm getting in the shower," Kane said, snagging his coffee mug off the counter as he walked by.

She grabbed his arm. "We're here if you want to talk."

He leaned down and kissed her forehead. "Thanks."

She watched him go. The casual expression on his face, the calmness in his voice didn't reveal how much this was affecting him. He was bottling it up, swallowing his anger and disappointment. Again. She'd rather see him fly into a rage.

"Go talk to him," she said to James.

"What for?"

"He needs somebody to talk to."

"I heard you offer and him say thanks. Talk over."

She rolled her eyes. "You're such a man."

James grinned. "Thank you."

She leaned toward him. "His father is *using* him for good publicity. He's hurt and angry. He needs his friends' support."

"He has our support. That doesn't mean we have to *talk* about it."

"Yes, we do."

"You're such a woman." Before she could argue, he went on. "And we don't know what Anton is doing here. Maybe he read that article, felt guilty and decided he really did need to show his son more support."

"Oh, you mean he's admitting he was wrong."

He frowned. "Okay, maybe not."

"But he feels guilty."

"Well, maybe not."

"Anton Jackson is doing what he does best—protect his image."

"Of course he is."

"You were ready to give him the benefit of the doubt thirty seconds ago. Why is that? Some football-star code of brotherhood?"

"No way, I—"

"That's how he gets away with the way he treats people, you know. Because he's a *star*." She slid off her stool and paced by the bar. "Fans clamor to get to know him. Women fall at his feet. He's coddled by his agent, his manager, his wife—everybody he encounters, in fact." She paused long enough to shoot him with a fond glare. "You and Kane would be the same way if you didn't have me to kick you both back in line.

"Of course, Mr. Superstar takes his fame and talent a couple of steps further. He stands in the spotlight like it's his God-given right. And all the while Kane tries to stand beside him, his father does everything in his power to keep him in the background. Plus, he makes sure everybody around him—and around his family—meets his superior standards. And that especially includes his son's girlfriends. Can't muddy up that exceptional gene pool with an inferior candidate."

When she fell silent, she found James staring at her. "Sounds to me like you were the one who needed to talk."

She dropped onto the sofa. "I guess."

"Been holding that in awhile?"

"Apparently."

"Feel better?"

"I think so."

"Good, 'cause here he comes."

Now dressed in his uniform, Kane appeared at the end of the hall. "You all right, Lex? You look like you're gonna be sick."

"I'm fine." She rose and glanced at her watch. "We need to get going."

When James trotted down the steps of the motor coach, Lexie snagged Kane's arm. "Are you going to defend him to the press?"

He stiffened but didn't turn to face her. "He's my father."

"That doesn't mean he's always right."

"I didn't say he's right."

"He doesn't deserve your respect."

"Yes, he does."

"He's here to save face with the press, not support you."

He finally turned his head. His eyes were glacial. "He came. That's all that matters to me."

Meaning, he was grateful for his father's attention and didn't want to rock the boat. She'd watched the same thing happen many times in the past.

"Lexie, we're not going to agree here. Just let it go."

"No. I'm tired of seeing him treat you this way. You need to confront him."

He jerked his arm from her grasp. "We need to get to practice."

CHAPTER NINE

"KANE, I UNDERSTAND your father is at the track today. How do you feel about him being here in light of this morning's newspaper article?"

Kane smiled confidently at the track reporter, though he felt anything but. "My dad's my biggest supporter. Of course he's here at such an important race."

"So there's no truth to the story that you and your father aren't close?"

"My father and I are as close as ever."

"Do you have any idea who on your team was quoted for this article?"

"No, I don't. But it was obviously somebody who doesn't know me."

"Thank you, Kane."

As Kane nodded, the reporter turned to face his camera. "Back to you, Ron."

Kane turned away and hoisted himself through the window of his race car. His stomach tightened. He hadn't lied. He'd respected his father. He'd kept his personal business to himself. A successful interview if there ever was one.

"Safe ride, buddy," James said as he handed him his helmet.

Kane nodded. He didn't want to talk about his father anymore, and his closest friend realized that.

Unlike Lexie.

He was still furious with her for her interference. She didn't understand. She'd never liked his father, probably never would. The differences in the way they saw him had always caused conflict.

Still, he respected her opinion and her loyalty. She'd always been one of the few people his father couldn't impress or charm into liking him. She saw his father's self-centeredness as a slight against him.

She must care about him a great deal to—

He smiled suddenly. "She's crazy about me."

"Who?"

Kane simply widened his grin.

"No. No way."

Kane put on his helmet. "No more blondes, buddy," he said, his voice muffled.

"I thought you were mad at each other. The temperature in the golf cart coming over here was frigid. And that's saying something for a vehicle with no doors or windows when it's eighty degrees out."

"It'll thaw."

"I really don't think—"

Kane cut him off with a thumbs-up and a flick of the master switch. He knew James didn't understand his focus on Lexie. Neither was he happy about the effect it might have on the team. Kane intended to prove his friend's fears were unfounded.

As he hit the track for practice, he put his personal thoughts aside. He concentrated on getting a feel for the car as it rolled around the wide, D-shaped track. He experimented with different lines, searching for the one that gave him the fastest lap times. He remembered to baby the brakes in Turns One and Three.

The car's setup was great, and he ran near the front the entire session. Harry and Lexie had really dialed this one in. Preparation, though, was only part of the battle.

They had to keep to their strategy for the race and hope cautions fell their way and wrecks didn't. It was a fun track for a driver to race, and he'd had more success than not in finishes there. But it only took one mistake on his part or another driver's—he recalled the Michigan wreck with a painful wince—to ruin everything.

The excitement of night racing and the beginning of The Chase hung in the air like the early-fall humidity. He was simultaneously nervous and exhilarated.

But he had miles to go before the race even began. He had a magazine interview to do, a meet-and-greet for another sponsor, the drivers' meeting, a team meeting and a meal or two to squeeze somewhere in between.

A pretty typical race day.

He'd barely get a chance to see his parents. It was no wonder they didn't come to races. He'd lost many relationships because of his job's time and focus and commitments, which made the married-with-children guys all the more amazing for finding a way to make their lives work.

"Any way I can squeeze in twenty minutes to see my mom?" he asked James as they walked away from the car after practice.

"I'm ahead of you there. Cookie, Inc. is catering dinner for the team in one of the sky boxes, so I put your parents on the guest list."

"Good thinking." He couldn't picture his elegant mother at an infield barbecue.

"That's what I'm here for."

"Where are we doing this interview?"

"The hauler." He glanced at his watch. "And we'd better get going."

"Can I have a word with you first?" Lexie said from behind Kane.

When they stopped and turned, he noted her eyes were shadowed by sunglasses, so he couldn't gauge her mood. He didn't want to go round two with her about his father, but he was such a sucker for her presence he'd take what he could get.

"Sure," he said, looking around in vain for a place on the busy pit road to talk.

"I'll go stall the reporter," James said, then jogg___ _ff.

"Let's walk," Lexie said.

It was still a little early for the fan mobs, b__ Kane still didn't see how they were going to stro__ to the hauler without being interrupted twelve time___.

"How about the pit box?" he suggested instead.

She shrugged, so he led the way.

They weaved through the crowd of mechanics, pit crews, reporters and other drivers—and got stopped twice by members of other teams—before they reached their pit and climbed the ladder to the box where Lexie and Harry watched the race and commanded the team.

He realized in that moment that his and Lexie's chemistry wasn't just personal. It extended to their relationship as driver and car chief. He'd spent a lot of the season aggravated when she pushed him, or told him he needed to find his passion before his career nosedived, but she'd been right about him suppressing his emotions too often. Her leadership was making him a better driver.

Smiling, he sat in the swivel chair next to Lexie. "Everything okay?"

"Yes. No." She waved her hand. "Everything's fine with the race." She took a deep breath and looked over at him. "I'm sorry I butted in earlier. Your relationship with your father is your business, not mine."

He laid his hand on her thigh. "I'm glad you care enough to worry about me."

She looked around apprehensively. "Kane, we shouldn't be doing this."

"Talking?"

"Touching."

"No one can see us up here."

"Except the members of forty-two other racing teams."

"They're not interested in us."

"Or the 4,236 cameras at the track."

"You're paranoid."

"Yes."

He leaned close and brushed his thumb along her jawline. "I thought we were discussing how much you care about me."

"You're killing me here."

He wished he could see her eyes. "I'm trying to arouse you."

"We have a race in a few hours."

"Don't we always?"

"I just wanted to apologize."

"I'm accepting."

"The flowers you left in my room were beautiful."

He hadn't sent a note, but he'd hoped she would realize

who the yellow and red roses were from. "Yellow is for remembrance. I looked it up. I added the red for luck—for the team and to remind you there are other couples in NASCAR who race together."

There were wives and girlfriends who played significant roles in drivers' careers. Back in the day, a lot of the wives even kept the scoring books for the teams. Lexie's job might be even more critical, but if those guys could manage it, so could he and Lexie. "Have you thought about dinner?"

"I haven't really had time."

"Especially since it takes so much effort to avoid me."

"I haven't been avoiding you. We've both been busy."

He stuffed his ego and reminded himself he couldn't expect her to spend every moment of the day thinking about him. She had as much, if not more, responsibility as he did.

She laid her hand over his, and his pulse jumped. "I'm trying to do my job."

"And I'm making it more difficult."

"Not on purpose. I just don't want our personal relationship to get in the way of the race."

He reached out and slid her sunglasses off her face. When her gaze met his, he saw the same warring emotions he'd seen for weeks in his mirror. Desire and responsibility. Longing and caution. She wanted him. She just didn't *want* to want him. "Do we have a personal relationship?"

"We could, but—" She glanced off in the distance. "I'm scared of falling for you, Kane. I can't go through that again."

"It'll be different this time," he said, though he wasn't sure himself. He just knew he was different.

And while he was sure he'd never be smart enough or sophisticated enough to measure up to her, he wanted to try. He wanted to make up for the past and see if their future could be one to share.

"Instead of dinner," he said, "how about a party at my house? To celebrate making the top ten."

"When?"

Whenever James can get things together. "Sunday night."

"Is the rest of the team coming?"

"Sure." A party with familiar people might take the pressure off their first official date in twelve years. "But I want you there *with* me." When she hesitated, he continued, "I need something, Lexie. I need something from you that convinces me I'm not making a complete idiot out of myself."

She had his body in a knot, his head spinning. He couldn't let her walk away from them again. They could make it work this time.

LEXIE KNEW she'd have to make a decision soon, and now the time had come. She'd been protecting herself—and the team.

But mostly herself.

"There's a lot at stake."

"I know."

She squeezed his hand. So many emotions rolled through her where Kane was concerned. They had a great deal of compromising to do to make their relationship work. A calmer, easygoing, more mature Kane would help make that happen. But could he be that man and still be a fierce competitor on the track? Could they have any hope of making a relationship work and still race together?

She thought of the warnings her father had given her earlier in the week, but ignoring her feelings certainly wasn't making them go away. And though no one would approve, and she might be making a serious career and personal mistake, she could no longer deny them a second chance.

If she got her heart broken again? Well, hell, it wouldn't be the first time.

"I'll come to the party," she said quietly. "For you. Not just for the team."

His eyes lit with pleasure. "Wear that black dress?"

She laughed, the warmth of his hand against hers infusing her with confidence. "I don't think so."

"You can take it off anytime you want."

It felt good to see his smile. The tension between them the past few weeks had made her forget how to relax with him. "No kidding. Anytime?"

He slid his hand higher up her leg. "Anytime."

"Hey, buster, that's still your car chief's thigh. You have a race to run, so you'd better get your mind back there."

His grin widened. "But my mind is happy where it is."

"In the gutter, no doubt." She stood. They both had a million things still to do. "What are we going to tell everybody?"

"Nothing. It's none of their business."

Skeptical, she stared at him. "You're not going to say anything to James?"

"Maybe him, and everybody else will find out eventually. But let's avoid your father. He, uh, warned me off a few weeks ago."

"Yeah? He did the same thing to me."

"Hey, Oil Man! Nice run!"

Lexie turned and looked down to see driver Bobby Cashman, one of their Hollister Racing teammates, walking by with some of his crew members.

"Stay off my bumper tonight, dude!" Kane yelled back as he stood. "I'm winning this one."

Cashman and his buddies burst into laughter.

Lexie watched them move farther down pit road, but she spoke to Kane. "You've *got* to beat him."

"He's a teammate. Shouldn't I cut him some slack?"

"You shouldn't cut anybody slack tonight."

"I know, I know. Fierce driving."

"Definitely. And keep in mind that I bet a hundred bucks on you with Cashman's crew chief."

He laid his hands over his heart. "Oh, baby, I'm so touched."

"And cut out the *baby* stuff. We're working."

"Yes, chief."

She shoved his shoulder lightly. "Go to your interview. I've got a meeting with my father, and some online shopping to do." She headed down the ladder.

"Shopping? *You?*"

She smiled up at him. "I wonder if Victoria's Secret delivers overnight?"

HOW WAS A MAN supposed to drive a race car at 180 miles an hour with forty-two other guys and think about lingerie at the same time?

How was a man supposed to concentrate on remembering the names of key executives at Cookie, Inc., as they hosted the prerace dinner for him and the team? How was a man supposed to answer his mother's questions about why the engines had to be so loud?

Simple. He wasn't.

Focus was as much a part of his job as breathing. Lexie knew this. Yet she still smiled at him from across the sky box as if she knew some secret he didn't. She'd twitched her hips as she climbed down that ladder this morning and had him fantasizing about what exactly she wore underneath her uniform.

Sunday couldn't come soon enough.

"I know about the big engines, dear," his mother said. "But why does it make that horrible noise?"

Damned if he could remember. He was too busy watching Lexie's glossed lips move as she talked to James.

"The fans like it," he managed to respond.

She shuddered. "They're all going deaf."

"Probably."

She glanced around the luxury sky box hanging high over the track, where his sponsor had set up a buffet dinner, bar and several TVs. "It's nice up here. Reminds me of the days after your father signed his apparel contract. It was quite a change from the players' wives' section in the stadium to being able to watch the games from the suites. You remember that?"

"Uh-huh." Lexie was sipping from a coffee mug, her lips closing around the rim.

"Of course these days, with all that money being thrown around, the players probably have their own boxes."

"Probably."

"It's really gotten out of hand."

Personally, Kane didn't have a problem with anybody paying him buckets of money to do what he loved. He doubted any lineman, quarterback or wide receiver for the Cowboys thought differently. "Mmm. I guess."

"How in the world did people survive without air-conditioning?"

"No idea."

"Are you listening to me, Kane?"

Perched on the arm of the sofa where his mother sat, he finally looked down at her. "Absolutely."

"You seem distracted."

"Just thinking about the race."

"Are you sure you're not losing your hearing?" his mother asked.

With considerable effort, he pushed Lexie out of his mind. "Yes. I wear a helmet and radio earphones."

"It must be ninety degrees out there still. Won't you get hot and—" she shuddered "—sweaty?"

He grinned. "Mother, you're such a girl."

She lifted her hand to the pearls at her throat. "What else would I be?"

He leaned down and kissed her cheek. "I was complimenting you. You're a lady. A true lady."

She flushed and slid her hand down the lapel of her lavender suit jacket. "A flirt. Just like your father."

Though he'd avoided his father during dinner, Kane directed his gaze to him now. *No. No, I'm not. But I think I might be okay with that for the first time in my life.*

He was much more impulsive and aggressive than his dad. But his control and maturity *had* needed work, and his dad had helped him with that. But Lexie was also right— his passion made him good at what he did.

Maybe he could succeed without being a copy. Maybe he could get to the top without being perfect. Maybe he didn't need to measure up to anyone but himself.

"Of course, he took the flirting in stride and acted like a gentleman. A loyal husband and father."

Deep down Kane knew that was true. His father loved the fame and attention, but he'd always honored his family.

He smiled at his female fans, he played poker occasionally with his teammates, but he hadn't fallen into the darker traps that financial windfalls and hero worship sometimes brought.

It was just that his focus on his son was for things he didn't want to do. Football. Public relations. Broadcasting.

Kane was lousy at all that, and he'd never understood why his father refused to recognize those realities.

He held his mother's hand. "I know."

"Have you seen that ridiculous newspaper article?" She sniffed in derision. "We'd planned this trip months ago. Your father spent hours on the phone rearranging his schedule to be here."

Guilt washed over him. His body went cold. He'd assumed, like James and Lexie, that his father had arranged a quick support trip after learning the article would be released. "Did he?"

"Disrespectful. That's what these reporters are these days."

"They're just doing their jobs."

"Humph. It's embarrassing. Make sure you tell him you appreciate him coming, you hear?"

"Yes, ma'am. The press will die down. Don't worry."

She squeezed his hand, then rose. "You're a good boy."

"I try."

"I think I'll have some wine."

Kane raised his eyebrows. His mother drank wine at Christmas, New Year's and the Super Bowl.

"I've hardly seen your father the last few months," she said with a twinkle in her eyes. "It's Saturday night, and I have him all to myself." With a sly wink, she glided toward the bar.

Good grief. That was way too much information.

But he couldn't help the warmth that spread through his

chest as he thought about his parents' love still going strong so many years after his mother had waved her pom-poms in the future-great Anton Jackson's face after NC State had decidedly trounced his North Carolina Tarheels.

Did he and Lexie have that kind of longevity and commitment?

He'd thought so at one time. But teenage idealism was a long way from the reality of making a relationship work for a lifetime. They'd decided to give their relationship another chance.

A lot of emotion stood between them, but was it enough? Or would the obstacles be too much to overcome?

After his mother left his side, his sponsor's guests surged toward him. He respected the distance they'd given him while he had family time, so he smiled even more broadly for pictures and signed autographs for them and their kids. One woman had brought her nephew with her. The ten-year-old was suffering from leukemia, and the prognosis was iffy.

Kane spent the rest of the party with the boy. There was no doubt the world had its share of suffering, but seeing it on the news and confronting pain in the face of a child was something entirely different. Every driver on the NASCAR circuit generously gave money and time to children's charities—by choice, not obligation.

"It's time to go," Lexie said, touching his arm as Kane watched the young cancer victim walk away with his mother.

"Yeah." Kane swallowed. The kids, sick or well, reminded him how lucky he was. He looked over at Lexie. "He's only ten."

She slid her hand down his arm to clutch his hand. "I know."

He let her lead him from the room. By the time they reached the infield, he became aware of her hand in his. The pall that had covered him faded. His fans and his team expected him to race his best, and he could do that, at the least.

"People are going to talk," he said to Lexie.

"Probably," she said, though she didn't release his hand.

They picked up James and Pete as they made their way to the car. They passed other drivers and team members. They got high-fives and some trash talking. Kane paused to sign a few autographs and talk with fans.

Lexie never moved from his side.

It was odd and encouraging. He wasn't exactly sure whether she was there as his car chief or his Saturday-night date, but he was grateful. The closer he got to the stage for driver introductions, the more nervous he became.

Their season was on the line. His reputation, respect within his family, respect among his fellow drivers, sponsor dollars, future sponsor dollars, the team's confidence, even everybody's jobs.

He knew the disappointment of failure. He'd never made The Chase. He'd never known that marketing boost, that validation. He wanted to succeed more than he wanted to draw his next breath. The Sunday-night party he wanted to have with Lexie was going to be over before it started if he didn't finish well tonight.

And it would all be decided in a matter of hours.

As each driver was introduced, cheers erupted from the stands. The track lights highlighted their ecstatic faces and colorful race wear. Fans and drivers alike loved Richmond. The cars went fast, and the drivers had to use every ounce of skill and ingenuity to make their way around the track and come home with a good finish.

"You'll be fine," Lexie said when they stood in their pit box next to the car.

Kane glanced up and down pit road. Other drivers were talking and laughing with their wives and girlfriends. Kisses and hugs were exchanged. Some prayed. It was an important, sometimes tense time for families.

He'd never trusted a woman enough to bring her into this circle, into this strange club where struggles and lost opportunities were as common as fame and fortune. His romantic relationships were short-lived and mostly superficial. He liked having Lexie beside him, even if no one else knew that the reason for her being there had changed.

"In fact, you'd better do *great*," Lexie continued. "That car I gave you is damn near perfect."

Smiling, he angled his head. "*Near* perfect?"

"Plus or minus driver error."

"Naturally."

She laid her hands on his shoulders and pulled him close for a quick hug. "Be careful."

"I will."

"I'll be there with you."

"I know." His nerves were fading in favor of anticipation. He could do this. *They* could do this. Together.

"It's time," James said as he approached.

Lexie squeezed his arm one last time, then backed away. The next time he'd hear her voice it would be on the radio.

When Kane climbed into the race car, his pulse was calm. Just another day at the office. It wasn't, of course, but it helped to focus on something normal.

"Hey," he said to James, "can you organize a party for tomorrow night?"

James grinned. "A top-ten party?"

"Just in case."

"I can throw something together. Anybody in particular you want me to invite?"

"If we make The Chase, they can all come." He waved his hand toward the thousands of rowdy people in the stands. "Other than that, the usual crowd."

"Women included?"

"Ah…no. Lexie and I are going together."

James looked as though he might argue, then he shook his head and laughed. "If anybody can make it happen, it's you and Lexie."

"I hope so."

James handed him his helmet. "Have a good race, man."

"Thanks."

As James turned away, Harry stuck his head in the window. "Relax."

"I am."

"Humph. Don't look relaxed."

"It's all on the line tonight."

"It's all on the line every week. Nothing special about tonight. Just another race to finish."

"And to place where?" Kane had asked this question several times of several different people and gotten blown off. No one wanted to freak him out and tell him he had to win to guarantee a spot in the top ten. And while he was pretty sure that wasn't the case, he knew the finishing number had to be high. The number went down in instances where higher-placed drivers finished badly, but he had no control over their races, so he wanted to know what he had to do. The worst-case scenario.

"Fifth gives us a guarantee."

"If I lead a lap?"

"Then sixth."

"What if—"

"Coddle those brakes, and we'll let you know what you need to do as the race winds down. It's gonna happen. I can feel it."

"Lexie thinks so, too?"

Harry nodded, his eyes narrowing. "You should know. You two are practically glued together."

His crew chief's respect was nearly as important to him as his own father's. On some level he was betraying that respect by not keeping his distance as Harry had asked him to.

"I think I'll shoot for the win," he said finally with a casual tone as if he'd just decided to go to the grocery store.

"Good idea," Harry said as he backed away.

To his surprise, his father leaned against the window. "Good luck, son."

"Thanks, Dad."

He clapped him on his shoulder. "No matter what happens, your mother and I are proud of you."

Kane swallowed hard, then managed a nod.

"Be careful," his father said before his hand slid away.

The last visit was from Pete, who was responsible for checking to be sure Kane was comfortable in his seat and all his safety equipment was fastened securely, before he patted the car off on its four-hundred-mile journey.

"Go for it, man," Pete said, slapping his gloved hand.

Kane gave him a thumbs-up.

"And, hey, we want you to make The Chase, but if you don't, you're still our guy."

"Thanks, Pete. Have you seen Mr. Hollister?" Kane had expected their owner to be pacing behind the pit wall.

"He told Harry he was staying in the sky box. He didn't want to put any more pressure on us."

"More than he already has?"

Pete grinned. "Yeah."

As he fastened the window net, Kane knew the time for reflection was over. Forward and counterclockwise was the only way to go.

"Gentlemen, start your engines!" roared through the track.

Kane exhaled and did just that.

CHAPTER TEN

"I'M LOSING THE HANDLING," Kane said as the silver Number 82 car streaked by him.

"You're doing fine," Harry said over the radio.

"I need tires."

"Next caution you'll get them."

Kane felt the car's back end slide. "We may not have that long."

"Hang in there."

Kane knew he was whining. He also knew he had to finish fifth.

Bob Hollister might have been harsh to warn them so close to the race about their jobs, but he had too many millions invested in the team to finish in the middle of the pack every week—where Kane had been the last three seasons. Many owners wouldn't have been nearly so patient.

Patience was *not* necessarily a good thing now, though.

Kane moved up the track slightly to keep the car behind him from passing. The fact that his car was able to do that gave him hope for the dwindling grip on his tires.

At three-quarters of a mile around, Richmond was considered a short track, but because of the high speeds, it had a superspeedway feel. It had hosted racing events for more than sixty years, before NASCAR was even founded. Fans and drivers alike loved the side-by-side, under-the-lights racing. Tires and brakes were everything, and when the rubber wore down, the cars tended to slide into the wall.

Just as Danny Lockwood had done on lap 152.

Given their stormy history and that Lockwood was twelfth in points, striving for that all-important number ten spot Kane wanted, he couldn't say he was sorry Lockwood was now limping around in the back, thirty laps down.

Kane rounded Turn Two, and the back end of the car slid again. "Whoa."

"Nice save," Lexie said, the relief in her voice evident.

Since she'd been silent for much of the race, it was comforting to hear from her. He was much more tense than usual, despite everyone's assurances.

"Trouble, Turn Three," his spotter, Bill, said.

Breathing a sigh of relief—tires were imminent—Kane slowed for the caution with the rest of the field.

As they rolled around the track and by the accident, he noticed Derrick Anderson's disabled car, looking too damaged to continue the race. His window net was down and the safety crew was already on scene, so Kane allowed himself a grin.

Derrick was ninth in points.

Somebody had to fall out in order for Kane to get in the top ten, and he was sorry it looked like it was Derrick. But he was also pumped.

"Pit next lap," Harry said. His voice was even, as if he had no idea of the significance of who'd caused the caution. He did, of course, but knowing Harry, he didn't want to jinx their fortune.

"What lap are we on?" Kane asked.

"320."

Eighty more. Could they stay in the game for eighty more?

He rolled into the pits, and the over-the-wall gang went to work. Somebody used a hook to hand Kane a fresh bottle of Gatorade, and they were off in 13.8 seconds.

"Position?" Kane asked as he slid into line with the other drivers and cruised back onto the track.

"Sixth."

They needed fifth. Or at least they had before Anderson wrecked. He didn't ask for an update on the points, and when the green flag waved, he focused on passing.

His car was strong on the fresh tires, and he was able to move up, but was he going to stop when he got to the clutch position and just hold his ground? Was he going to be just good enough, or was he going to act like a champion?

He clenched the steering wheel.

He was fighting for his team and he wasn't yielding an inch until he crossed the finish line, fighting to be the winner.

THIRD. THEY'D FINISHED THIRD at Richmond.

They were in The Chase.

Before the winner—the points leader, Patrick Williams—even finished burnouts on the front stretch, the media descended into the Sonomic Oil pits.

"Lexie, are you relieved to be so instrumental in finally getting the team into The Chase?"

"I'm not sure how instrumental I am, but—"

"The team never made it into the top ten before you arrived."

This wasn't going to become a thing, was it? Dear heaven, she hoped not. She had enough going on at the moment.

From watching her father deal with the press—and

going through her own blitz at the beginning of the season—she knew it was best to say as little as possible. "Everyone at Hollister Racing is thrilled. We've pulled together like never before to make this happen for Kane and our entire team. We'll shine in the final ten races."

"Being the only female car chief in NASCAR NEXTEL Cup racing, do you feel a special validation for having made that elite group of ten?"

"I think women are making great strides in NASCAR, but anyone would be excited about their team being in The Chase. It's been a team effort, so we're all proud of what we've accomplished."

"Are you personally proud of your driver?" one guy asked.

Despite the tabloid world of today, most sports reporters were reluctant to ask personal questions unless your personal life directly affected the sport you were involved in—i.e. you were a big basketball star and got married on the court before a playoff game.

But there were still moments where personal and professional lives merged. It was common knowledge she and Kane had once dated. Rumbles of speculation had followed their pairing in the garage, years after their breakup. What would be said if—or when—their private reunion was public knowledge?

Then again, it wasn't much of a reunion yet. They were going to a party together. Which she'd decided to do less than twelve hours ago. Did she actually think the media was *already* interested?

Laughing at herself, she waved away her paranoia. "Yes, I'm proud of Kane, as well as our entire team."

Thankfully, her father walked up at that moment, saving her from further speculation.

"Harry, how do you feel about making The Chase? Do you think your experience will help your driver over the next ten weeks?"

Always impatient with the media or anybody, her father narrowed his eyes at the reporters. "I think my driver can handle himself just fine. Did you see that save on lap 315? It wasn't me steering that car."

"But it has to be comforting for Kane and the rest of your team to know you've been to the top. You know how to respond to pressure."

"But I'm old. Believe me, I'm as grateful to have my team—and my daughter especially—as these guys might be to have an old guy's experience on their side."

Though it seemed a lifetime since the race ended, Kane's car pulled up in the pits. James and the rest of the team descended on him as Lexie and her father pulled away from the reporters and let them surround their driver.

"We did good, Dad."

He laid his arm around her shoulders. "We've got a helluva team."

Lexie's heart skipped a beat as she watched Kane hoist himself out of the car. His smile could no doubt be seen from the heavens. She couldn't hear his words, but she watched his lips move.

She'd had some serious fantasies about those lips in the past few weeks. She'd have him all to herself tonight. Well, after all the team congratulations, the media interviews, the trip to the airport, the flight home…

So maybe not tonight.

But tomorrow night…

Hmm, not exactly then, either. The party would be crowded with friends and team members. They'd all want to relive the great moments of the last few races. She'd hardly get Kane to herself.

And as much of a temptation the attention the black dress might bring was, she knew she wouldn't wear it. The party was a *team* celebration. Drawing attention to herself would be tacky.

IF ONLY THAT INCLINATION had somehow found its way to Cheryl Tolfort's thought process.

Instead of the low-key, I'm-just-here-to-support-the-team entrance Lexie'd planned the following night, Cheryl had talked her into a red tank top and skin-tight jeans.

"I don't know about this," she said to Cheryl as they pulled up to Kane's lake house.

"Would you stop? This is what people wear to parties."

"You left out 'normal' people."

"I was trying to be encouraging. I thought we got past all this shyness stuff last week."

"That was in front of total strangers. This is my *team*."

Cheryl rolled her eyes, then slid out of her SUV, slamming the door behind her. Lexie had little choice but to exit her side of the car.

During the pit celebration last night, Kane hadn't seemed to care what she wore. He'd hugged her against his chest, kissed her temple and assured her she was the greatest car chief NASCAR had ever known. Then later, in the confusion of everyone boarding the plane, he'd *really* kissed her in the shadows.

Normal people, she guessed, would actually have their date pick them up, but further proof that she was far from normal occurred when Cheryl called that morning and demanded to take her to the party.

Glancing down at her cleavage peeking over her red tank top, she now understood why.

"I won't get any respect dressed like this," she said as they trudged up the driveway toward the house, which was lit like Daytona on the Fourth of July weekend.

"So? Good grief, Lexie, you don't have to wear your Beta Club badge on your chest twenty-four hours a day." Obviously frustrated, she turned, laying her hands on Lexie's shoulders. "Being attractive and wanting to impress the opposite sex doesn't make you an idiot. Do you think *I'm* stupid?"

Lexie's jaw dropped. "Of course not. You run that front office like a general *wished* he could run a war zone. Why—"

"I'm blond. I'm busty. I like to remind people I'm both."

Lexie saw where this argument was going, but was reluctant to see how it applied to her. "But you don't work with guys."

Cheryl raised her eyebrows. "Really?"

"Well, ah…you don't work on technical…"

"Have you ever seen one of those brilliant engineers of yours try to work the fax machine?"

"Ah…no."

"It's not pretty."

"Okay, okay, so they respect you, and you're still—" she glanced at Cheryl's black minidress "—still you. But I'm not you."

"No, but you don't have to pretend you're not a girl to have respect."

Lexie looked up at the house and remembered the first time she had driven by, just after she'd heard Kane had moved in. She'd imagined him heating up frozen pizza in the oven.

He'd never been much for sophisticated food. For the prom, they'd eaten with several other friends at a fancy restaurant in downtown Charlotte—after which he and James had claimed they needed a cheeseburger if they were going to make it through the night.

As his car chief, she'd been to the house a few times, but obviously never as Kane's date.

Still, she'd seen a few of the women in Kane's life. They dressed like lingerie models. She'd never been too impressed, and guessed by the brevity of their relationship that he hadn't, either. But she couldn't imagine having the confidence to smile and banter the way they did. To cock her hip and angle her head in just the right way.

Cheryl seemed to mirror her thoughts. "Catch their attention with your bod, then keep them with your brain."

"You're starting to scare me."

"Yeah?"

"You're making sense."

"Let's go."

"Still…why does it have to be so public? Why can't we get a corner booth in some dark Italian restaurant, where nobody knows us?"

"Are you always this much trouble?" Cheryl asked, though she obviously didn't expect an answer, since she grabbed Lexie's arm and led her up the steps to the front door, which was wide open. "Not much on security, is he?"

Come one, come all. It was so Kane. And James.

Half the neighbors surrounding Lake Norman had probably invited themselves. But since most of them earned their living in one way or another via NASCAR, she supposed they'd all be one happy family.

As they entered the foyer, they were instantly enveloped

in the crush. To the right in the dining room, the table was covered with party food—wings, chicken fingers, chips and salsa. Several people holding red plastic cups looked as if they'd found the keg several times over. They'd no doubt be calling cabs before the party wound down. At least the neighbors could just stumble home.

Tim Butler, one of the other Hollister Racing drivers, swayed toward her, then buzzed her cheek. "Are we awesome, or what?"

All three Hollister teams had made The Chase. No other owner had achieved that feat. And since Bob Hollister was such a well-respected man in racing, she doubted anyone begrudged him the windfall.

As they moved toward the back of the house, they ran into many more people they knew, including members of their own team and veteran driver Mike Streetson, whose tanned, weathered face and mischievous smile always made her think of the Gulf fisherman near the beach house she and her father used to rent at Christmas each year.

When she and Cheryl reached the kitchen, they found Pete acting as bartender.

His eyes flew wide at the sight of Cheryl and her spectacular curves. "Something I can get you ladies?"

"Not beer," Cheryl said, wrinkling her nose. "You have any champagne?"

"You bet." He winked, his attraction to Cheryl obvious. "This is a classy joint."

He served her a glass in an actual flute—which James must have rented for the night, as Lexie couldn't imagine Kane owning champagne glasses.

"And what can I get you?" he asked, turning to Lexie,

his gaze drifting down her body and lingering in places it certainly wouldn't in the garage or on the track.

"You do remember I'm your boss, right?" Lexie said when his gaze finally landed back on her face.

"Oh. I—" His face flushed, and he cleared his throat. "Oh, right. Champagne?"

"Sure."

"You look really…nice," he said somewhat hesitantly and not meeting her gaze as he handed over the wine.

"Thanks."

"Ignore her," Cheryl said with an eye roll in her direction. "She's repressed."

"I am *not*."

Cheryl smiled. "Prove it."

Knowing full well she was being dared into seeking out her date, Lexie gulped half the glass of champagne, then rolled her shoulders. "I'm going outside."

After sliding through the crowd, she walked through the open sliding-glass doors and onto the back deck. The spectacular view always stole her breath for a second or two. The sun was setting behind the trees in vivid colors of orange, pink and purple, and the receding light dotted the lake like diamonds.

The back of Kane's house was its strength. The builder had constructed a series of multilevel decks with custom designs carved into the cedar railings. The decks spread out wide, then ventured close to the water's edge. The grotto-style pool was nestled on the right side of the house, surrounded by tropical foliage, featuring natural-rock waterfalls, fountains, a hot tub and artful lighting.

Dozens of people talked and laughed in small groups.

Some had settled in the lounge chairs by the pool. Everybody seemed to be having a great time.

By contrast, nerves jangled in Lexie's stomach. She'd eaten very little for dinner, and the gulp of champagne was making her head swim. She set the half-full glass on a table that had collected several other cups and plates, then swallowed her anxiety and searched the decks for Kane.

If he could get in that car each week and face the track and all those other drivers, she could do this.

It's a party. You're supposed to relax.

Okay. She could do that. According to Cheryl, she was dressed for a party. She had a date. She'd had a drink—well half of one.

But instead of Kane, she saw her father, which naturally reminded her of work and not relaxing all over again.

"Hey, Dad," she said, embracing him.

"Hi, sweetie. You look…nice."

Nice again?

Wasn't a woman supposed to look, well, *hot* for a date? But then she didn't want her *dad* thinking she looked hot. He might drag her home, like the night he had in junior high when she'd shown up at the track in a skintight miniskirt and halter top.

Probably not the moment to bring that up again. "Thanks," she said. "How long have you been here?"

"Just a little while. I was about to go home."

She linked hands with him. "Stay. Everybody's here. You'll just go home to an empty house."

He sipped from his beer bottle. "Yeah. Maybe."

He didn't look like a Chase-making crew chief. "Are you okay?"

"Yeah." He sighed. "The real work begins now, doesn't it?"

Real work? What the devil had they been doing the last twenty-six weeks? Slacking?

"Can we enjoy this for at least twenty minutes?" she asked, knowing she sounded like James.

"It's been twenty-four hours."

"Come on, Dad. Everybody needs this. We've been killing ourselves the past few months."

"Humph. Gonna be nursing hangovers in the morning."

"You gave everybody tomorrow off, remember?"

He hunched his shoulders. "Shouldn't have."

She smiled. Though he didn't say it, she knew he was so proud he could burst. The more taciturn he got, the more touched he was.

And despite the career boost everyone from her to Kane to the crew got from landing in the top ten, there was a great deal of satisfaction for her father, as well.

Being a crew chief had changed so much over the past twenty years. Her father had gone from chief mechanic to personnel manager. He'd transitioned from the stopwatch era to multimedia computers and real-time diagnostics. To most, the move appeared seamless. Lexie knew it had been anything but.

Her father wasn't a computer guru by any means, but he'd learned enough—from her and others—to understand the process and the data and, as a result, hire the right people to make the team mesh and succeed.

"You're amazing," she said, hugging him briefly. "I'm going to mingle."

"You are?"

"Yeah. You should try it."

He grabbed her hand. "You're going to find him."

She met his suspicious gaze without flinching. Kane had asked her not to tell her father about them. But, like everything in racing, she didn't see how they'd keep it quiet for long. "I'm going to mingle."

With a wave, she descended to the midlevel deck. There she found the rookie whose mistake had wrecked Kane at Michigan. He and his girlfriend were ridiculously awed to meet her. They both looked fifteen, renewing Lexie's insecurities.

Kane had loved her at seventeen. Twelve years had passed since then. Her mother had been married with a child by this age. What was she doing here in jeans and a red tank top and looking for a date with a man who could literally pick any woman he wanted?

Strong arms embraced her from behind. "Hi," Kane said in her ear.

She closed her eyes briefly and breathed in his scent. There was something so right, so reassuring about his touch. His nearness made her tremble.

"Hi," she said as she glanced over her shoulder.

His blue eyes, bright with pleasure and anticipation, focused on her face. "When did you get here?"

"Just a few minutes ago."

"Oh, my God, you're Kane Jackson."

Suppressing a laugh, Lexie turned back to the rookie's girlfriend.

Introductions were made, the rookie flushed even deeper, and Kane wound up signing the girl's plastic beer cup with a Sharpie she produced from her jeans pocket.

Just as Lexie was about to question whether or not the girl was even legal to drink beer, Kane gripped her hand

and tugged her away. She noted he was wearing faded jeans and a black polo—and looked *amazing*.

As they descended the next set of steps to the pool deck, she couldn't help noticing the way the jeans hugged his lean hips. She was so used to seeing him in his uniform—which, admittedly, left little to the imagination regarding his body—that seeing him in civilian clothes did strange things to her pulse.

Another bar had been set up on the pool deck. Kane got her another glass of champagne and himself a beer, then he dropped into a lounge chair and settled her next to him, her legs draped over his.

"Comfy?" he asked, tapping his plastic cup against her plastic champagne glass, which somebody had thoughtfully provided for the pool area.

"I, uh…" She stared at his meltingly handsome face and tried to swallow around her dry throat. "Sure."

"Nervous?"

"Of course not."

"Yes, you are."

"What do I have to be nervous about?"

"Me. You like me, and you don't want anybody to know about it. Least of all me."

"Maybe you should have asked your ego to this party."

"It's too much to handle. You, however…" His eyes darkened as he slid the back of his hand across her cheek. "Are just right."

Her stomach quivered. He had her so off balance she couldn't think straight. "People are going to talk."

"No kidding? That'll be a switch."

"I'm serious."

He pressed his lips against her jaw. "So am I."

Unbidden, her eyes fluttered closed. She was pretty sure she'd gone crazy. She *knew* he was crazy. But a nuclear explosion couldn't have pulled her away from him.

"Are you going to relax now?" he asked against her cheek.

She looked up at him. "I'm a puddle at your feet. Do I have a choice?"

"No." He raised his cup. "How about a toast?"

She raised her own glass. "To the top ten."

He shook his head.

"To the team?"

Another shake.

She pressed her lips together briefly. "To us?"

He smiled and tapped his cup against hers. "And our future."

EVENTUALLY KANE LOST Lexie's exclusive attention.

As with any racing gathering, a small crowd formed on the pool deck to remember past races and share old glories. To everyone's delight, Lexie and Mike Streetson shared stories about her early days at the track, when he used to drive for her father's team.

Kane watched the tension and uneasiness fall away from her face as she talked. He loved seeing her laughing instead of consumed by the pressure of her job. He'd nearly swallowed his tongue earlier when he'd glanced up at the deck and noticed her standing there in a red tank top and curve-enhancing jeans. With her hair falling in a smooth curtain to her shoulders, she looked soft and approachable, not like the all-business crew chief everybody jumped to attention for.

And while his ego liked making her nervous, deep down he wanted her as comfortable being his date as she was being his pit road guide. Streetson and racing stories were familiar to her, making her forget the double takes they'd been getting for the past couple of hours.

He'd known they were going to be news, and he should have expected Harry's cold shoulder and other members of the team goggling like they'd seen a car take flight in Turn Two. His own father would also have some choice words for him about his lack of focus and professionalism, along with the perils of dating a colleague.

Well, too damn bad. They were all going to have to get used to seeing him and Lexie together. He had no intention of letting tonight be a one-time event.

"Remember when that goofball Ricky Matthews tried to steal the Martinsville clock trophy back in '93?" Streetson said to Lexie.

"It's kind of hard to forget," she said dryly. "He used me as a lookout."

"You gotta hear this one, guys." He gestured with his cup. "Let me just get another beer."

"I'll get it," Kane said as he leveraged himself off the lounge chair. "You want anything?" he asked Lexie.

She glanced up at him, and the friendly laughter in her eyes immediately heated. She licked her lips. "I'm fine. Thanks."

Fine with what? Kane dragged his gaze from her glossy mouth. What had he asked her? What was he about to do?

"Get movin', kid," Streetson said. "My throat's drying up over here."

Oh, right. Beer. He started off in the direction of the bar, wondering what he could drink to get his heart to stop its out-of-control gallop.

"Hey, Alex," he said to the team jack man, who was filling his own cup from the keg.

"Hey, K. Great party."

"Everybody needed it." Kane filled Streetson's cup, then his own. "Wanna join us?" he asked, nodding his head toward the crowd around Streetson and Lexie.

Alex shook his head. "I'm looking for a woman."

"Anybody in particular?"

"Nope. I'm not picky. Where did you find that foxy woman you're with?" he asked with a comical leer.

"I—" He stopped, realizing Alex meant Lexie. "That's Lexie."

Alex squinted. "Nah."

"Yes."

Alex patted him on the back sympathetically. "I think you oughta lay off the beer, buddy."

As he walked away, Kane wondered why Lexie was unrecognizable without her uniform and ball cap. No one seemed to have any trouble drooling over her at the sponsor party at Bristol. Maybe it was just that no one could imagine them together. They probably thought he wasn't smart enough to interest a brain like Lexie.

You sure didn't hold on to her before.

Yeah, well, this time was different.

He returned to the group and handed Streetson his beer. "So Matthews decided his car was crap, but he wanted one of those grandfather clocks Martinsville gives away as a trophy."

"Hey, everybody," Pat Williams said as he walked up. "Congrats, Kane," he said, holding out his hand.

Kane leaned around Lexie and shook his competitor's hand. "Thanks. You, too." After his wreck at Michigan,

"The Hatchet" had fought his way back to first in points. Everybody said he was the man to beat, and now Kane was one of the drivers determined to do just that.

They were casual friends and hung out sometimes, racing go-karts or playing computer games, but for the next ten weeks they'd be pitted against each other on the track and in the media. Kane was glad James had invited him and they had this moment of calm before the storm landed full force.

"Pull up a seat," Kane added, indicating the chairs scattered alongside the pool.

"You bet." He dragged a chair over, and others in the crowd scooted to make room.

"Am I ever going to get this story out?" Streetson asked the group in general.

"Yes," Kane said. Anything to keep Lexie smiling.

"So we've got Matthews and a clock," Streetson said, leaning forward. "In those days they kept the clock in this storage closet behind one of the concession stands. The lock on the door was just a plain old Master padlock. A pair of bolt cutters would take care of things easy. But the track did have a security guard, who supposedly had this big, mean dog go on patrol with him."

"They probably paid him in hot dogs," Pat said.

"Must have been a stout dog," one of the guys in the crowd added. "Those things are lethal."

Streetson shook his head. "Great minds think alike. Matthews figures if he encounters the dog, he can toss a couple of hot dogs its way, giving him the chance to escape. He even hires a lookout." He looked over at Lexie.

"Hires? The jerk blackmailed me."

"Oh-ho," Pat said with a grin. "Straitlaced Lexie has a skeleton in her closet? Wanna share?"

She exchanged a flushed glance with Kane. "Ah, no."

"He'd caught us making out behind Streetson's motor coach," Kane said, caught between amusement and exasperation by her embarrassment. "He threatened to tell Harry."

Streetson snorted. "As if he didn't already know."

After another quick, guilty glance at Kane, she said, "He said he had *pictures.* The letch. It's one thing to know, entirely another to *see.*"

Before Kane could question her about these pictures he hadn't known existed, Streetson continued. "So Matthews and his unwilling accomplice head to the trophy's storage shed, where he's planning to cut the lock, then load the clock on a dolly." He raised his eyebrows. "By himself, I mean to tell ya, obviously not realizing that clock must weigh three hundred pounds."

"And I'm supposed to whistle if I see the guard coming," Lexie added. "Of course, I'm looking for the guard so I can tattle and go back to bed."

"Poor guy," Pat said. "The plan was flawed from the start."

"Matthews is hard at work with his bolt cutters," Streetson continued. "For any normal person this would be like cutting cardboard with the kitchen scissors, but Matthews weighs 110 soaking wet."

"He made Barney Fife look hefty," Kane added.

"Well, the break-in is taking some time and eventually the guard and his dog get around to the storage shed. Matthews's lookout—" He nodded at Lexie.

"Is long gone."

"So it's a big shock to our thief when the dog starts barking. And soundin' real close.

"And here, my good friends, is where the story splits

into the Matthews version and the real version. In the Matthews version, he ducks behind a post, waiting until the dog and the guard are just a few feet away. Then, heroically, he jumps out from behind the post, charges the dog and the guard, tosses the hot dogs, then does some kind of fancy footwork and escapes before either man or beast even thinks about chasing him."

Streetson shook his head. "When he tells me and my team all this the next morning, we figure most of it's bull. Since we were working with a rain delay, we decided to find the guard and get the real story. According to him, Matthews tossed the hot dogs all right, but the guard dog caught them in the air in one gulp, then charged. Matthews freaked out, turned and ran. The dog caught him in three strides and chomped down on his butt."

As his audience roared with laughter, Streetson added, "The guy had to sit on a cushion during the race. Plus, the guard was so proud of his pooch's crime foiling, he insisted on showing us a picture of Bitsy. It was a stinkin' poodle!"

"In all fairness, it was a *big* poodle," Lexie said.

"It was a *show* dog," Streetson said. "Had those silly looking pom-pom things all over its head, tail and legs. Any man who runs from a dog that looks like that deserves to get bit in the butt."

"So the clock was saved?" a woman in the group asked.

"Yep." Streetson smiled. "And it looks pretty nice sittin' in my den."

Though he knew the story well, Kane laughed along with everybody else. Many of his friends and teammates were younger than him and new to NASCAR. To have a legend like Streetson pass on stories about the good ol' days, to have a driver of his caliber sitting a few feet away, sharing a beer with them like buddies, must be a surreal experience.

It certainly was for him every time it happened.

The stories crowd swelled, then diminished. At one point, Lexie excused herself from the group. When she didn't come back after several minutes, Kane went in search of her.

He found her by the lake, staring into its moonlit depths.

Even her silhouette was inspiring. He swelled with pride as he imagined her standing by his side. The tip of his fingers tingled with the urge to stroke her skin, to hold her in his arms and absorb her touch and inhale the fruit and coconut scent he couldn't seem to put out of his mind.

He desired her as he never had another woman. He longed for her respect as he never had another person.

Could he really be a strong enough man for her? With all his faults and shortcomings, his past mistakes and the ones he'd no doubt make in the future, did he even deserve her?

His own father didn't respect him. How could he expect Lexie to?

He closed his eyes briefly and forced himself to walk closer, banishing his insecurities and doubts. "You never told me Matthews had pictures," he said as he approached her.

She didn't turn around. She'd no doubt sensed him there long before he'd spoken. The woman didn't miss a thing.

"He was probably bluffing. You know what a talker he was."

"Are you thinking about him?" he asked, stopping just behind her. Ricky Matthews had died of a stroke just a few weeks ago, no doubt prompting her and Mike Streetson's memorial by storytelling. It was the way of a Southerner. The way of racing.

"No." She turned her head to look at him. "I was thinking about you."

He smiled. "Yeah?"

She faced him, laying her hand on his chest. Her gaze flicked to his mouth, then back up to his eyes. Her eyes glittered with longing and promise. "I never got to really congratulate you for making the top ten."

He could already taste her on his lips. His chest tightened in an effort to draw a deep breath. "We ought to do something about that."

Her lips curved. "Yeah, we should."

Their mouths met gently, with promise and need. The future and the past were both prevalent in their minds. So much was at stake.

But he concentrated only on her, on the way she made him feel, on the way he wanted her to feel. They'd given so much of themselves to their jobs, to other people and other aspirations. They deserved to enjoy each other.

When she pulled back, she was breathing hard. "I should probably go."

He held her tighter against him. "Don't. Don't go."

She stroked her fingers through his hair and smiled.

CHAPTER ELEVEN

WRAPPING HERSELF in a throw from the end of the bed, Lexie padded to the balcony off Kane's bedroom. She sat on the porch swing and curled her feet beneath her, staring out over the dark and silent lake.

Right or wrong, she and Kane had taken an irrevocable step forward tonight.

Being held in his arms was as wonderful as she remembered. And just as burdened with problems.

Their careers and reputations were seriously on the line now. As teenagers they'd worried about their fathers catching them, but young love had made them bold and blind to any true consequences. Now there was no denying the risks they were flouting.

Maybe Kane wasn't worried. Racing was a wild, risky profession. Was she just another risk to take? Another challenge to overcome?

She had to prepare for that possibility, but she knew, regardless of his feelings for her, she'd gone and done it again—fallen hard.

Fast. Sure. Completely.

Without him she was pretty sure she wouldn't draw another easy breath. With him she wondered if breathing would be even harder.

She'd longed for an accountant, a lawyer, a waiter. She'd gotten none of those. As a teenager, she'd fallen in love with a race car driver, and, truth be told, she'd never fallen out.

With a quiet giggle, she pushed aside that practical, think-of-everybody-before-yourself side and indulged in happiness. A long time had passed since she'd felt this content. As she basked in the glow of reunion, she remembered a time when she and Kane had been wrapped in each other's arms as young lovers and looked out on this same lake.

They'd shared so much together. The disappointment of his football days dying. The birth of his enthusiasm for NASCAR. The hopes for their future together. The sadness when their love had been overwhelmed by careers, jealousy, arguments.

She'd lost the love of her life, but somehow she and Kane had formed a new bond. She felt the same in some ways, and completely different in others. Her emotions were all over the place—blissful, exhilarated, worried. They'd changed and grown up, but would things really be better this time?

Could Kane love her? Real, true, deep love? The love of his life?

"Can't sleep?" he asked softly.

She turned to see him standing in the doorway, his hair wavy and mussed, wearing only his jeans. She swallowed hard and had to look away before she could answer him. "I'm just thinking."

"Regrets already?"

"No," she answered truthfully. She didn't regret. She dreaded.

Big difference.

But with him so close and their renewed intimacy still

lingering in the air, she had no intention of dwelling on her fears at the moment. She held out her hand. "Join me?"

He cast a glance back—at the bed, no doubt—then sat on the swing, pulling her back against his warm chest.

"It's quiet," she said.

"Probably why so many drivers live out here."

"You?"

"Yeah. The isolation is nice." He stroked his fingers down her bare arm. "And sometimes lousy."

She recalled many Sunday nights she'd sat on her own back porch and wondered where everybody had gone. After the buildup to race day, all she had left was her own company. "The loneliness in our business, alongside so much intensity, is hard for a lot of people to understand."

"Not you."

"Only because I've been a part of it for so long. Sometimes I wonder what it would be like to have a normal life," she added quietly.

"You'd rather have a nine-to-five job?" he asked, his surprise evident.

"No." What would she do if she didn't spend all her time either working on cars or going to the track? The idea was as likely as flying to the moon.

"You ever think about what you'll do after you retire?" she asked.

"No."

She glanced back at him, but the night shadowed his expression. "Yes, you do."

"My father thinks I ought to do PR for the NFL."

She stiffened. Conversations about his father were always loaded with tension. And, as was typical with Anton Jackson's suggestions, she completely disagreed.

She'd never known anybody less likely than Kane to work in public relations. He was great with the fans, but he was also impatient. He was terrible at organization and worse at playing politics. Plus, he would never get anywhere on time if James didn't schedule every minute of his weekend.

He surprised her by smiling, then kissing her forehead. "I can read your thoughts, you know."

She raised her eyebrows. "Really?"

"Oh, yeah, you're thinking you haven't heard a worse idea since Ricky Matthews suggested you be the lookout for his clock-stealing scheme."

She laughed and turned slightly, laying her head against his chest. "Pretty close."

He stroked her hair. "I like having you here."

"I like being here."

"Are you sure?"

His heart thumped beneath her ear. Doubts and worries pushed her to confess their concerns, but she ignored them. "Yes."

"You seemed uncomfortable earlier."

"I didn't see any point in broadcasting our relationship—past or present."

"We were among friends."

"I'm not ready to share us with them, either."

"You're embarrassed."

Startled, she lifted her head. "I'm not." She cupped his jaw, then pressed her lips briefly against his. "I'm not at all. It's just that once everybody knows we're…"

"Sleeping together."

She winced. "Too much information. I was going to say *reunited*."

"You don't want anyone to know we're sleeping together."

Hearing the angry, wounded tone in his voice, she sat up straight. "Once everyone knows about us, the speculation, the truth, whatever…it'll become a *thing*."

"A thing?"

"An excuse for why you're driving great. Or not so great. A reason why I'm happy and made the right adjustment on the car. A reason why I'm annoyed and forgot to double-check the ignition box. Then it's not about us anymore. It's about everything else. We're entitled to a private life."

"I don't want to apologize."

She slid her thumb across his bottom lip, which was entirely too firm. "I'd never ask you to."

"You did with Victor Sono."

He was their primary sponsor. They couldn't afford to annoy him. There was nothing personal about her request. "I was a car chief then," she said.

"You're not now?"

"Definitely not."

She kissed the corner of his mouth, reassurance welling up in her as she realized how nice it was to touch him, to not be constantly holding back. She wanted to relive their longing and passion over and over again, until he was again familiar, until she'd memorized every sigh and touch. "Remember what we did the night we sneaked out to your parents' lake house?"

"Vividly."

"You wanna do that again?"

"I think I could be persuaded to go there."

She wrapped her hand around the back of his neck and pulled his head toward her lips. "Go there."

AFTER FINISHING SIXTH in the first Chase race at New Hampshire, Kane arrived in Dover on Thursday night with a surge of confidence.

Which lasted about ten minutes.

Apparently, Lexie had told her father she was staying with Kane in his motor coach this weekend.

When they got to the track, they'd rushed to the hauler for a brief meeting with Harry. And his crew chief—the man who'd been his mentor for too many years to count—gave him one long, hard stare, then ignored him completely.

He'd talked to his daughter about race details and the car setup, but not with his usual easiness and affection. His anger and disappointment was evident.

Lexie had warned Kane this would happen. She'd told him a lot of people were not going to be happy for them and had convinced him last week to say nothing about their relationship. She'd also refused to stay in his motor coach with him.

But he had no intention of hiding from anybody.

He wanted her to stay with him, despite her dire warning that the team was going to worry about how their relationship would affect the team, their communication and chemistry. Their friends were going to worry they would be pushed aside. His female fans, according to Lexie, were going to hate her.

Kane had dismissed most of her concerns. Until now, anyway.

What was *with* people? Didn't they have anything else to worry about? *He* wasn't entitled to a slice of happiness? *He* wasn't supposed to have a private life?

He stalked out of the hauler and paced outside. Looking back on his lunch with James yesterday, he remembered even his best buddy still had reservations about him and Lexie dating again. He'd asked Kane how things were going, as if he expected trouble.

Did they think being with Lexie was going to affect his driving? Like Samson cutting his hair, he'd suddenly forget how to press the gas pedal? That he'd get on the track and wonder whether he should go right or left? Surely they'd all settle down once everybody realized how ridiculous that was.

If anything his concentration should improve, since he wasn't focusing on his conflicts with Lexie anymore. He'd had a great finish last week, and that seemed like proof to him.

He'd just have to act as if nothing had changed. He wasn't into public displays of affection, anyway, but he'd make double sure he treated Lexie professionally in public. He'd make sure he treated all the guys the same—though he couldn't imagine why he wouldn't.

The door opened behind him, and Lexie stepped out. "Ready to go?"

"Sure. How did—" He stopped when he saw tears glimmering in her eyes. Immediately the no-PDA vow died. He drew her into his arms. "What did he say?"

"The usual parent stuff—you're making a mistake, you're ruining your life."

But Harry wasn't a usual parent. In all the years he'd known them, he'd never heard him and Lexie fight. A reunion with him, however, had provoked an argument that ended with her in tears. Not exactly a confidence booster or a mood destined to keep the spark alive in their romance.

Why couldn't they share their happiness with the people who meant the most?

He sighed in disappointment and hugged her against his chest. He'd caused a rift between her and her father. He'd pushed her and pursued her. He'd convinced her nothing would change except that he'd finally be able to look into her eyes and be honest in telling her he no longer wanted to just be her friend and teammate.

His chest tightened when he considered that it wasn't just any man involved with his daughter that upset Harry. It was him personally.

Was that just because of their positions on the team, or did the resentment go deeper than that? His own father had never fully accepted him and the choices he'd made. Harry always had. Would his relationship with Lexie cost him that respect?

"You wanna dump me again?" he asked her, striving for humor.

Sniffling, she clutched him tighter, her face pressed against his throat. "No."

"But you told me so, didn't you? You told me everybody was going to freak out."

"I did tell you so," she said, her voice stronger.

"But then, you're always right."

She lifted her head and looked up at him. A tentative smile hovered on her lips. "I must really be pitiful if you're conceding that."

"I concede nothing. I was trying to make you laugh."

"Doesn't make me less right."

"Depends of the subject. Gear ratios?"

"Mine."

"Wind tunnel statistics."

"Mine again."

"Pass protection in football."

She wrinkled her nose. "You can have that one."

"What about…" He whispered a naughty suggestion in her ear.

"Oh, well, okay. You get that one, too," she said, her tone husky.

He kissed her gently. "I'm sorry you and your dad argued."

"Yeah. Me, too."

"You want to talk about it?"

"Later. I'm starving." She tugged his hand, and they headed to his motor coach.

There they made dinner together, then watched a sitcom on TV. Tomorrow he'd have to share her, so tonight he planned to be greedy. Shades drawn, and the rest of the racing world shut out, they made love on the sofa. Each time he held her he was reminded of the precious gift she was to him. He could very easily fall in love again.

Not just teenage infatuation, but the happily-ever-after kind that changed a man forever. The kind of relationship that had him wondering about building a family and changing anything in his life necessary to keep her happy and devoted to him.

Was he already there?

As she moved around in the kitchen making a cup of tea, she wore only his T-shirt. Her hair was tousled, her face relaxed. He'd never seen a more beautiful sight.

But when did you *know?* Did you just look at a woman one day and know?

She's the one. I want to spend my life with her.

He'd have to remember to ask his dad. Despite the years that had passed, the struggles of life and the temptations encountered by a famous athlete—and the man had the Dallas Cowboys Cheerleaders hanging around—his parents were still very much in love. They understood and supported each other. They connected on levels he had no concept of.

He knew Lexie's parents had had that same kind of relationship, though they'd been cheated out of their lifetime together. He'd never understood until recently how much that mattered.

"He doesn't think I'm good enough for you," he said, not even realizing the thought had entered his brain until the words emerged from his mouth.

Lexie looked up, watching him from over her mug. "He's got on his crew chief cap," she said, obviously not needing an explanation for who *he* was. "He's pissed off that I'm distracting his driver."

"You're not distracting me." He grinned, his gaze sliding down her half-bare body. "Well, you are, but he's upset about more than me driving his car."

"He's jealous. I'm the only woman in his life. He doesn't want to share me."

"He said that?"

"No, but that's the heart of his issue." She rounded the bar, then sat beside him on the couch, her bare legs curled next to his jean-clad ones. "That and not wanting to see us fall apart again."

"Who says we're going to fall apart?"

"Nobody said we're *going to*. He just worries that *might* happen."

"We've been back together less than two weeks, why—"

"Is that what we are? Back together?"

"Sure, what else?"

Her gaze flicked up to his. "We've had one date, a couple of sleepovers, and now we're spending the weekend together."

"Right."

"So we're exclusive?"

What else would they be? "Yes. You have other plans?"

"No. Just checking. And you didn't ask, by the way."

He furrowed his brow. Was she annoyed, or just messing with him? "You want me to ask you to go steady?"

Smiling, she set her mug on the table. Then she turned to him and curled her hand around the back of his head. "Oh, Kane, how sweet. How traditional."

Messing with him. Definitely. He slid his arms around her. "How about if I offer you my senior ring?"

"I never gave it back."

He frowned. "You didn't?"

"No. It's still in my jewelry box."

"You didn't burn it or toss it out of a fast-moving car?"

"Of course not." She blinked innocently. "Thought about it a few times."

"Well, I feel loads better, and you're distracting me from my point." What *was* his point? Touching her was always distracting.

Harry. Not good enough. Ah, falling apart. "Do we have to spend every moment reliving past mistakes?"

"Hey, you asked. He remembers how hurt I was before. He considers you the cause of that pain."

"I was."

"It was a two-way street. I let a lot of things bother me that I wouldn't today."

"Like…"

LEXIE LOOKED DOWN, then back into Kane's eyes. She'd been teasing him, but the issues were serious ones. She shouldn't still be carrying baggage from the old days. "I was unsure of myself, and I didn't like the other women who hung around. I was jealous of the time you spent in the garage. Your dedication to racing. I always felt I was second. A very distant second. I realize now that's just part of who you are. It's something I have to accept."

He stroked her cheek. "Racing isn't first, and you aren't second. You don't have to accept leftover time from me."

For a long time she'd dreamed of hearing those words from him. Were they really true now, or had they been true before and she'd just been too insecure to see them? She wasn't sure, but she hadn't imagined his distraction and his restlessness when they were together.

One thing she knew—they were both young. Could things be different this time? Could she be more confident? More demanding when she needed to be? Could he be less impatient off the track and still be aggressive on it?

Other than nearly knocking Danny Lockwood on his butt at Bristol, he'd certainly found a good balance between driver and man off the track.

He'd listened to her advice and understood she wasn't criticizing but helping. The younger Kane never would have done that. He would have lost his temper, and they would have fought, or he simply would have walked away from her. His track performance was benefiting. The cautious driver she'd started with in February at Daytona had been replaced with one of smart ambition.

"I was lousy at balancing things before," he continued. "I'm better now."

But he still had an unquenchable desire to win, for hard-charging competition—every driver did. And he still had a desperate desire for his father's respect. For his father to see him as an equal. She wasn't sure that would ever happen, and she wasn't sure how that affected every other relationship in his life.

She couldn't turn away from him, though. Regardless of her father's warnings, of her own internal doubts, she'd thrown her heart into the ring with Kane Jackson again.

The risks were like debating the success of a two-tire pit stop. Smart for some. Stupid for others. And a complete crap shoot for everybody in between.

"The next nine weeks are the most important of our professional lives," she said.

"And we're going to succeed. Together."

"It's going to be complicated."

"It wasn't before?"

"It could get messy."

"It wasn't before?"

She threaded her fingers through his silky hair. "Your optimism is inspiring."

"It helps at 180 miles an hour."

"But you still don't think you're good enough."

Shadows passed through his eyes. "The track is different."

"No, it's not." She pulled him close, until their lips were a breath apart. "You're good enough—no matter what. Don't let anyone tell you different."

He kissed her, but before the top of her head spun off, she managed to pull back. "So if we're exclusive, that means I'm your girlfriend, right?"

He trailed his lips along her cheek. "Right."

"Does that mean I can punch out those chicks who drool all over you at meet-and-greets?"

Smiling, he leaned back. "I thought you said you'd grown beyond that."

I lied. "Can I at least *think* about punching them out?"

Considering, he angled his head. "Are these women carrying licensed merchandise?"

Oh, good grief. Merchandise—aka model cars, T-shirts, caps, coffee mugs, pillows, watches, et cetera—he made money from the sale of. Every driver's retirement plan. As part of the NASCAR community, however, she *was* opposed to bootlegged goods. "Fine. Only the ones with unlicensed stuff."

"No kids."

"Did I say anything about kids?"

His eyes laughing and bright, the shadows gone, he pulled her into his lap. "Deal."

THE NEXT DAY Kane walked through the hauler to the small room at the back that they used as an office/locker room. "Can I talk to you?"

Hunched over the desk and staring at a computer screen, Harry didn't even look up. "We've got qualifying in a few minutes."

"It's important."

Sighing, Harry took off his cap, scratched his head, then leaned back in his chair. "So talk."

Reining in his temper at the impatient look on his face, Kane rolled his shoulders. "Lexie and I would appreciate your support."

"For?"

Kane ground his teeth. "Us seeing each other." And if he asked *when,* he was going to lose it.

"I'm sorry. I can't give it."

"Why not?"

"The timing is lousy."

"The timing will always be lousy."

"It's bad for the team."

"I can't live to please the team."

"It didn't work out before."

"We were young before."

Harry's eyes narrowed. "You hurt her."

"I know, but she's willing to forgive me. You can't do the same?"

He said nothing for a long time, and Kane felt the weight of his choices—both past and present—bear down on his shoulders. He'd made mistakes in not working as hard on his relationship with Lexie as he had on his cars. He'd been too selfish to notice her struggles. He'd been too impatient to succeed.

He wasn't that guy anymore.

"She's my only little girl, Kane," he said finally.

"I thought you trusted me."

He folded his hands and looked down at them. "I'm worried about her. She...cares about you."

"Lexie isn't some weekend conquest for me."

Harry met his gaze. "She isn't?"

Kane turned away, trailing his hand through his hair. His chest tightened. He couldn't believe this was happening. That he and Harry had come to this impasse.

After all they'd been through, Harry didn't trust him, didn't respect him or want him anywhere near his daughter.

"I've made mistakes in the past," he said finally. "But Lexie means the world to me. Always has."

He stopped short of the *L* word. As much as he wanted to convince Harry of his sincerity, he didn't fully understand his own feelings, so he didn't see how he could share them with anybody else. Maybe Harry sensed his uncertainty. Maybe his concern was justified.

He turned back. "Just give us a chance. Lexie feels your disapproval, and I don't like seeing her upset any more than you do."

That blow obviously landed. Harry's hands clenched. "It's up to her to give you a chance. I won't lie and tell her I like any of this."

Kane forced himself to relax his jaw so he could speak. "If you can't support *us*, I'd appreciate you supporting Lexie."

"I'd appreciate you not telling me how to treat my daughter."

Kane absorbed a blow of his own. The personal connection he'd always had with Harry was crumbling, and it was clear neither of them intended to back down. "I'm sorry I bothered you," he said, then turned and stalked from the room.

CHAPTER TWELVE

KANE'S HEART POUNDED as he crossed pit road and headed to the wall separating the team from the car during the race. The smell of engine oil and gasoline washed over him, comforting him with its familiarity.

Chemistry was so important to a racing team. The interaction between the members was often the difference between winning and losing, between finishing well and sliding into the wall on the last lap. The Chase had barely begun, and his team's chemistry was imploding as a result of the tension between Kane and Harry. And while he felt like he'd already had a successful season by making the top ten, he didn't want to rest there. He wanted to win. More and often. He wanted the championship.

He also wanted to punch something but didn't. He wanted to scream but didn't.

He'd spent much of his life working on control. Because he was a fierce competitor, or because he just lacked patience?

Since qualifying was about to get under way, he sat alone for no more than a few minutes, but the time allowed him to control his thoughts and emotions.

"Great party the other night," Mike Streetson said as he walked up and sat beside him.

"Thanks."

"The pressure getting to you yet?"

"Yep."

"You belong here, you know. Just keep doing what you've been doing all season."

Without access to Harry, Kane felt directionless and alone. Knowing he was the cause of conflict between father and daughter, guilt was piled on top. "Don't think I can."

"Success changes people, Kane. It affects the dynamics of the team. It changes personalities, goals and expectations. You wanted to make the top ten. You have. Now what?"

How did he tell the man and the driver he admired so much that racing had very little to do with his problems?

"You go for it all, that's what," Streetson continued in that quiet, determined way he had. "It's any man's championship. Just because you've never been here before doesn't mean you won't be the one hoisting that trophy in December."

"I'm the only one of the ten who's never been there."

Streetson scowled. "Doesn't matter. Stay focused. Keep your team up and motivated. If you can't win, get a top five. If you can't get top five, get top ten. Be smart. Save your engine, your tires, your brakes. Be there at the end. This game is about consistency, not just a celebration in Victory Lane. Don't forget that."

But he still felt like the guy who'd skated in, who didn't belong but had somehow pulled out a last-minute miracle. What Streetson was trying to remind him of was that miracles were the stuff of NASCAR legend.

His father was the legend, though, not him.

"My father would do it."

"Hey, we all make our own way in the world. You can't define yourself by other people. *Especially* people you're related to."

"But if I fail, the world knows." He hunched his shoulders. "And comments."

"Oh, I know you're not going to fall back on 'Oh, poor, pitiful me.'"

Kane sighed. "No, I'm not. Truth is, my driving isn't what worries me. It's Lexie."

"She's a great car chief. What—"

Kane said nothing, but he could see the wheels in Streetson's brain turning. "Who you were awful close to at the party. Who you used to be even closer to."

Kane nodded.

"This is personal."

His stomach pitching in the same weird fall he'd felt when he and Harry had argued, Kane nodded again.

"Mmm, well, that makes things sticky, doesn't it?"

"Oh, yeah."

"I don't have to tell you racing is just as much mental as physical. And your personal life plays a part. Still—"

"Sir? Mr. Streetson? Could you sign this?"

Kane and Mike looked up to see a young boy with a model car held out and a hesitant smile on his face.

His mother stood behind him, her hands on his shoulders. "I know you're busy, but…"

Streetson waved away her apology with the ease of a veteran and took the car from the boy. "What's your name, son?"

"Michael."

Streetson smiled and set his Sharpie into motion. "Like me, huh?"

"Yes, sir." The kid's smile was wide, and he was all but dancing on the tips of his toes. "I think you're the greatest driver ever."

Streetson handed back the signed car and winked. "You'd be right."

Kane watched the exchange in silence, never resenting the attention his friend got and admiring his smoothness and confidence. "How do you get past that?" he asked when the boy walked away. "How do you agree you're the greatest driver?"

"I don't agree all the time. But do I think I'm still good enough to win? Hell, yeah. I prove it every once in a while. And I'm definitely not ready to hang it up. I see the end coming, but I'm gonna fight like crazy until then.

"And until then the fans keep me going. The fans buy sponsor products. The sponsor dollars keep us racing. Simple as that. And when I feel like crap, when I'm hot and tired and want to just get the hell out of some broke-down, wrecked, ill-handling race car, I remember those kids. You do, too. Otherwise, I wouldn't bother myself to talk to you."

"Harry isn't happy."

"I imagine not. You're way too close to his little girl for his comfort. Forget he's one of the best crew chiefs ever. He's a father."

"I get that. I tried to talk to him."

"No go, huh?"

"No way."

"Give him time."

"We've got nine weeks."

"Harry's a professional. He won't let this affect the team."

"How can it not?"

Streetson grinned as he rose. A man who'd seen it all, done it all. "Avoiding him as much as possible couldn't hurt."

Right. He's my crew chief. Maybe I should ask one of

the other Hollister teams if they'd mind me pitting over there during the race.

"And, Kane?" Streetson said as he turned back.

"Yeah?"

"Don't go looking at *my* daughter. I'd hate to break up our friendship."

Well, now he felt loads better.

He couldn't deny he understood. If he ever had a daughter, he wasn't sure he'd want her involved with a pedal-to-the-metal race car driver. But being the driver in question was beyond frustrating.

As Lexie handed Kane a Sharpie, he shifted his beer bottle to his left hand and sent a flirtatious smile her way.

The VIP crowd assembled in their sponsor's sky box was mostly people they'd met many times before, but somebody always showed up needing an autograph for Aunt Susie, or a guy who'd decided he needed a signature to prove to his third-grade teacher, who thought he was a sure-fire loser, that now he was a bigshot.

The sky box was carpeted in plush navy blue, with TVs hanging in the corners near the ceiling for visitors to view the action on the track. Furniture was artful, tasteful and plush. The men were dressed in business-casual khakis and polo shirts. The women wore designer clothes, and even the ones who went with a more casual jeans look had diamonds encircling their wrists and fingers. Even the kids were decked out in polished duds—though the looks on their faces were as eager as any kid at a local dirt track.

The buffet included prime rib, sautéed shrimp, caviar and delicately cooked vegetables prepared by world-renowned chefs. Crisp white tablecloths covered the tables.

The lighting was gentle, the air filled with the scent of gently roasting meats.

Somehow, Lexie perversely longed for the heat, grease and noise of the pit road.

How far things had come from when she and her father had started. From the days when crew chiefs were tire changers, and the NASCAR awards banquet had taken place in a hotel in Daytona Beach instead of the grand ballroom at the Waldorf-Astoria in New York City.

The growth of NASCAR beyond the South had brought them attention, had enticed her father to come clear across the country from California and challenge the status quo. Though they'd been met with some resistance, having not been born in the bedrock of the sport, most everyone had eventually come around. They'd recognized her father's dedication and yearning to be schooled in the NASCAR way.

Today, with drivers, crew members and owners coming from every part of the country, this seemed silly, but Lexie remembered a time when they were rebels and newcomers. When multicar teams were an anomaly, rather than the norm. When engineers were met with skepticism, instead of a "hey, maybe these boys have something." When *the boys* meant only the men instead of a generic term for the team. When not having a Southern accent made you stand out as the minority—well, *a bit* more than now.

NASCAR was surging again, and everybody was uncertain.

Pretending she was nothing more than a helpful crew member, she smiled as Kane signed the autograph. While she, Kane, her father and James mingled with the crowd as the NASCAR Busch Series race roared along the track below, she reflected that she was doing more and more of that lately.

Pretending. Smiling when she'd rather not. Swallowing her words when she'd rather argue.

Part of her understood this was a reflection of success. Nobody wanted to upset the gravy train. Nobody wanted to be the one to make noise. To make a mistake and be blamed for their failure.

And she was certainly included.

Lexie was beyond hurt by her father's reaction to her and Kane. She was pissed. She normally liked watching races, especially when she could evaluate from the sidelines without a vested interest in the outcome. Plus, Hollister Racing was going through a number of drivers, giving them each a five-race audition to join them for a complete season next year.

She liked watching the up-and-coming talent. She enjoyed talking to those drivers and sharing their excitement. She'd even gotten to the point in her career that the guys asked her advice about certain aspects of the sport.

But the tension tonight made her edgy and irritable. Despite the excellent buffet and rare opportunity to relax, she'd much rather retreat to Kane's coach, go over her lap times and strategy for tomorrow's race.

"You might want to make an appointment with the dentist."

Lexie turned her head and glared at James. "What are you jabbering about?"

"You're gonna need some dental work after chewing all those nails."

"You're not cute."

He waggled his eyebrows. "Sure, I am. All the ladies say so."

"Not this one."

He laid his arm across her shoulders. "Love isn't supposed to be painful, you know."

"Really?"

"I could have saved you—if you'd listened to me. This whole business was doomed from the start."

"I thought you were one of the two people who actually approved."

"I was trying to be a supportive friend, but—" He frowned. "One of *two*? Don't you mean three? You, me and Kane?"

"That would be two—you and Kane. I think this whole deal is headed for disaster."

"You can't go into a relationship with an attitude like that."

"Why not?"

"That's the guy's job."

"Well, then, blame all these men I'm around all the time."

"Think positive."

"Why?"

James grabbed her elbow and pulled her into an empty corner of the room. "We have wine, food, women and racing."

Glancing across the room, Lexie saw two women pointing and whispering in their direction. "I think that benefits you more than me."

James looked beyond her, smiled widely, then sobered as he focused on her again. "Lexie, I really don't think—"

"This is the beginning of a beautiful relationship? That's helpful, since this isn't the beginning by any means."

"You are your father's daughter. Always thinking the worst."

"Thanks, I—" She stopped because though normally she'd be thrilled to be compared to her dad, today she wasn't. Her dad's habit of considering the worst that might happen helped him win races, but it wasn't helping their relationship. He was being stubborn and inflexible, negative…like her.

As much as she resented his lack of acceptance of her and Kane, her attitude was just as lousy. Lexie didn't believe they would last.

There were so many obstacles in their path. While Kane desired her, he didn't love her, and she wasn't sure he ever would. She'd challenged him and incited his competitive spirit by telling him they shouldn't go out. Now that he had her, the initial rush would be gone. How would he feel about her in a week? Or a month?

Her heart kept urging her to go full force, to give her love fully and take a chance again. But past hurts made her wary. And negative.

The phrase *doomed from the start* ran through her mind.

Yet she didn't know how to combat her feelings of dread. As a woman, she wanted so much from Kane—passion, undivided attention and commitment. As a car chief, she wanted those things, too. But he certainly couldn't give her and racing undivided attention. If he was dating someone else, she'd tell him to quit thinking about romance and focus on his job.

She was at war with what she wanted personally and what she knew was best for her team.

For nearly all her life, her family and her career had gone hand in hand, which was why she was just as much at odds with her father as she was with herself.

He was right. Dammit.

He hadn't been graceful about the delivery, but he was right.

"Give yourself a break," James said, chucking her lightly under her chin. "You don't have to take on the responsibility for the entire team."

Astonished, she stared at him. "Yes, I do. That's my job."

"How about not for tonight? Ignore your father, have some fun and relax."

"I can't relax. We have nine races left. The championship—"

"Will still be there in the morning."

He took her hand and practically dragged her to the bar. "She'll have a martini."

"No, she won't."

The bartender, who didn't even look old enough to serve drinks, paused with a silver shaker in his hand and looked to James for direction.

"A cosmo?"

She shook her head.

He sighed. "Wine?"

"I guess."

The bartender still looked hesitant, but finally set down the shaker and withdrew a wineglass from his cart. He poured the Chardonnay James selected.

"You could be less predictable," James said to her.

"I will. Tomorrow, when it counts."

"PIT STOP IN EIGHT LAPS," Harry said through the headset in Kane's helmet. "We'll take a pound out of the rear."

"That's too much," Kane said, roaring into Turn Three of Dover's Monster Mile.

"And we'll take two out of the front," Harry continued as if Kane hadn't spoken.

Kane ground his teeth. The tension from the night before had gotten worse during the race. Harry spoke to him in clipped, hostile tones and ignored his comments about the car. Despite his attitude, they had been in the top ten most of the day. Kane attributed the success to his ability to keep cool despite the poisonous surroundings.

But he'd been pushed back as far as he could go.

"*Half* out of the rear and *one* from the front," Kane said, his voice tight with strain.

"One and two," Harry countered.

Well aware anybody at the track with headphones, including the media, plus anybody with an Internet connection, could hear him, Kane tried to stay calm. "I don't want that big of an adjustment. I don't need it."

"We didn't adjust enough when we were here in June. That's why we came in twentieth."

"We don't need it."

"You're getting it."

Not the conversation to have at 130 miles an hour.

Kane shifted his grip on the steering wheel and did something some people wouldn't have thought possible a few years ago. He swallowed his pride and said nothing.

"Screw it," Harry said. "I'm done."

Then there was silence.

The silence dragged on, somehow drowning out the roar of the forty-three race car engines. Kane's heart pounded as if he was running around the track instead of driving around it.

Had his crew chief just dumped him in the middle of a race?

The next voice he heard was Lexie's.

"Kane, we've got three laps until the pit stop. We're taking half a pound out of the rear and one out of the front."

The directions he'd given. Where was Harry? Why had he stopped talking?

"Harry?" he asked carefully, unsure what was happening.

"Ah…he stepped away for a moment. Didn't feel well."

Several emotions rushed through Kane. Disappointment, anger, confusion, more anger.

"I'm here," Lexie added.

She was calling this, in other words. On her own. Without Harry. He'd *stepped away*.

Given up.

Lexie's fears had come true. She was sure they wouldn't be supported. She'd been afraid their relationship would affect the team.

They weren't. It had.

He was furious on so many different levels, he didn't know which one to attack first.

They were without a crew chief. Temporarily or permanently?

Somehow, Lexie held it together. She kept the pit crew motivated and everybody else calm and controlled. They rolled along like nothing out of the ordinary had occurred. With the pressure they'd all been under, maybe they thought Harry really had gotten sick.

A delusional person should probably not be driving a race car, but buying into that fantasy was the only way Kane could keep his composure and concentrate on the race.

They finished ninth, and all Kane could think about as he drove into his pit stall was pulling Lexie into his arms. As he climbed out of the car, though, the tension and pressure were evident on her face. She was barely holding on.

He noticed Mike Streetson, whose pit was just a few stalls down, heading toward his hauler. "Hang on," he said to Lexie, squeezing her elbow, then he jogged over to his friend.

"Mind if Lexie and I tag along for the ride home?" he asked, after congratulating Mike on his seventh-place finish.

"Yeah, sure. You in a hurry?"

"Uh, yeah."

Streetson slid on his sunglasses and grinned, his white teeth standing out starkly against his deeply tanned face. "Then you're in luck. Back here in fifteen?"

"We'll be here. Thanks, man."

He hurried back to Lexie, feeling as though he'd cleanly taken another hurdle in a seemingly endless race. While Kane relied on the Hollister Racing plane to get him to races, Streetson owned a personal jet that either he or one of his pilots flew to every event—either sponsor promotion, interview or race. With a guaranteed finish in the top ten this year, Kane had earned a nice bonus and could suddenly see the reasoning behind such a large expense.

"Get your stuff," he said to Lexie in a low voice when he returned to the pit. "We're going with Streetson."

"I have to help load—"

"I bet your father is feeling better and can handle the loading."

She crammed her hat farther down on her head. Her face was flushed with anger. "It's my job. I can't leave."

Undeterred, Kane glanced around. The team was already breaking down the pit like a smooth ballet. They'd had a good race, but everyone was anxious to get home after a busy weekend. He finally spotted James, standing by the hauler doors. "James!"

James hurried over. "Nice race," he said, toasting him with a water bottle.

"Thanks. Do you mind watching over things here? Lexie and I are going home with Streetson."

With his sunglasses on, James's expression wasn't clear, but Kane knew his friend had caught on to the need for a quick exit without further explanation. "You bet. But I'm taking Monday off."

"Yeah, yeah."

"This really isn't necessary," Lexie said. "I'll handle the loading. You guys go with Mike."

Kane snagged her hand and pulled her against his side. "You're coming with me."

She dug in her heels, obviously about to argue.

"Please? For me?"

"You really think I'm that much of a sucker?"

"I hope so."

She sagged against him. "You're right."

"I'm going to shower and change," he said, feeling his heart lighten for the first time in hours. "I'll be right back."

"I need a shower, too, you know."

"You'll have one." He winked. "At my place."

ON THE FLIGHT HOME, they shared a beer with Mike and didn't mention Harry once. Mike, as always, was full of great stories that distracted them from the race they'd just run and the crisis they'd have to face Monday morning.

When they reached Kane's house, he pulled her wordlessly into his arms. He didn't really want to deconstruct the day, though he doubted she'd let things be until morning. Still, simply grateful for her strength and presence, he absorbed her familiar feel and scent.

"Our team is falling apart," she said as they stood in the foyer, the moonlight sliding through the front door's etched glass.

"No, it's not. We held it together."

"For how long?"

"As long as it takes."

"He'll probably resign in the morning."

"Then we'll figure out a way to win without him."

"We can't. I—" Her voice hitched. "*I* can't."

He cupped her face and stared intently into her eyes. "I won't let you give up on this team. Or us."

She closed her eyes. "I'm just so tired."

"Come on." He held her hand and led her up the stairs. "I'll start a bath for you, then you can get some sleep."

He felt incredible satisfaction from taking care of her. She, who always thought of everyone else's needs but her own, let him take the lead and let him coddle her. It was a building block to having her trust him again, to believe in their relationship again. He was determined, somehow, to hold the scattered pieces of his world together.

And the next morning, wearing only his T-shirt as she stood in front of his stove, making a mess of a ham and cheese omelet, he finally coaxed a genuine smile from her face when he told her she might know about race cars, but she definitely needed some pointers with a skillet.

The bliss lasted right up until the moment the doorbell rang.

CHAPTER THIRTEEN

"KANE? YOU UP, SON?"

Poised with a spatula over an omelet, Lexie froze at the sound of Anton Jackson's voice echoing down the hall.

"He has a key?" she whispered incredulously to Kane, her heart leaping to her throat.

"My mom likes to bring casseroles to put in my freezer."

She glanced down at her T-shirt and bare legs. Talk about awkward.

"Kane!"

"In the kitchen, Dad! It's fine," he added to her in a quiet voice. "We're adults, remember?"

Funny, but she didn't feel like an adult. She felt like a teenager caught necking the backseat of her dad's car.

"I smell breakfast," Anton said, then ground to a halt when he reached the kitchen and caught sight of her. *"Lexie?"*

She smiled weakly. "Want an omelet?" There'd be plenty, since she felt nauseous all of a sudden.

"I—" Anton shook his head. His gaze darted to his son. "How long has this been going on?"

None of your business was the answer that came to Lexie's mind, but she said nothing.

"A couple of weeks," Kane said.

Anton's expression turned from shocked to thoughtful, bordering on calculating. "Who else knows?"

Kane shrugged.

"Who *else?*"

Lexie's embarrassment was fast giving way to anger. Anton had no right to barge into Kane's house and demand answers about his personal life. But then it wasn't her house or her father. She'd backed down and burst into tears when her own dad had questioned the wisdom of her dating Kane. Maybe they could switch parents. Kane could take her dad, and she could take Anton.

In fact, she'd like that immensely. She'd take great pleasure in taking Mr. Hall of Fame down a notch or two.

"A few close friends," Kane said. "But I'm sure it'll be common knowledge soon. We're not hiding."

Anton dropped his head and sighed. "You can't go out with a member of your crew," he said, as if this was obvious.

Which it was, as Lexie had often pointed out. Though neither she nor Kane had listened.

Kane crossed his arms over his chest. "I can. I am."

"The marketing people at Sonomic won't stand for it, and what do you think Bob Hollister is going to say?"

"They can't tell me how to live my personal life."

"Sure they can. They pay the bills."

Lexie knew Kane was on the edge of losing it, and she could hardly blame him. Being confronted with the truth was hard, and she was getting a strange sense of déjà vu.

"They don't run my life," Kane said, his tone growing harder, the muscles in his jaw jumping.

"It's bad for PR."

"I don't care. I'm not you."

"I don't expect you to be me," Anton said, his eyes growing frosty. It was clear he didn't appreciate his son's belligerent attitude.

Many times Lexie had wished Kane would tell his father off, or at least to mind his own business, but now that the confrontation was happening—and she was the cause—she felt lousy and selfish.

"I expect you to have respect for your career and for your team," Anton continued. "You don't need this distraction now."

The smoke alarm shrieked through the room, and Lexie rushed to the stove to deal with the now-crispy omelet. Her heart pounded as Kane and his father continued to argue behind her.

She'd been so busy worrying about the team, she hadn't even *considered* Bob Hollister discussing her love life with his staff, other executives, sponsors and heaven only knew who else.

Her cheeks burned with humiliation. She'd worked so hard to be taken seriously, to always be professional, to excel in a male-dominated world. Was she risking all of that? Had she really expected *this* much drama over her and Kane?

"Come on, Kane," Anton said, breaking into her thoughts. "You know how racing works. Your reputation is everything. You're the center of a multimillion-dollar ad campaign. Everything you do affects that—what you say and how you say it, your personality, your lifestyle."

"Who I date shouldn't matter."

"It does." Anton cast her a look she might think was actual regret from anybody else. "I'm sorry, but it does."

The déjà vu grew stronger. She recalled the party in the suite during the NASCAR Busch race, when she'd realized that though she was angry at her father, he was right.

Anton was right. Both of them were right.

And Lexie was light-headed.

"I don't appreciate your interference," Kane said.

"You've always welcomed my advice before."

"You always give it. You don't ask if I want it."

"I'm your father. It's my job to guide you."

By now the two men were just inches apart. Dark and light. Older and younger. Scruffy and polished. Their expressions of rage were the only things that matched.

"I'm not you! I'm never going to be you."

"I've never asked you to be."

"You expect me to do what you'd do. You always have. You've never supported my racing."

Anton took a startled step backward. "That's not true. I never stood in your way—even though you only started racing to defy me, so you wouldn't have to play football."

"I was terrible at football."

"You could have been great! If you'd given it a chance, if you'd tried harder."

"I tried! But I hated it, I hated every single minute of being compared to you, knowing I'd never, *ever* measure up."

"I can't control what other people said," he whispered. "I always encouraged you to do the best *you* could do."

"My best wasn't good enough. You know it wasn't."

Anton cupped the back of his neck, as if trying to rub away the tension of the increasingly confrontational discussion. "Is that what dating a teammate is all about—defying me? Doing something I would never consider?"

Lexie felt the blood drain from her face.

Kane paused in answering just long enough that the idea grew in Lexie's mind, spreading like poison. Was Kane using her to get back at his father? Did he really want her at all?

"Don't be ridiculous," Kane said.

Maybe he wasn't doing it consciously. But on some level Lexie knew it was true.

She'd never believed she and Kane would last, so why was she surprised? Why was her heart pounding and her stomach hollow?

"Lexie?"

She blinked and focused on Anton, who had seated himself at the bar running the width of the kitchen.

"You haven't said anything," he said to her. "Aren't you concerned how you and Kane will affect the team?"

Kane watched her but said nothing. He already knew she was worried. But while she agreed with Anton, there was no way she was siding with him in front of Kane and humiliating the man she loved.

"We've done pretty well the last two weeks," she said.

"Will it last?"

Considering they had already cost the team the best crew chief in NASCAR, she didn't see how. And she decided she liked Anton Jackson even less when he *was* right, instead of just always acting like he was right. "This isn't a conversation I want to have wearing only a T-shirt. I'm going to change."

Kane grabbed her arm as she strode from the room. "I've never seen you run from a fight," he said quietly.

She couldn't look him in the eye when she said, "Then this is a first, isn't it?"

In Kane's bedroom, she stripped off her T-shirt and rushed toward the bathroom, bypassing the rumpled bed and fighting not to think about the intimacy and affection between her and Kane that she'd become used to so quickly.

She snagged her clothes from the bathroom floor, put them on, then stuffed everything else in her overnight bag.

Her throat was tight, but she refused to give in to the threatening tears. She was a professional, and it was high time she started acting like one.

Taking a deep breath, she headed toward the stairs. At the top, she paused, noticing Kane standing at the bottom. She continued more slowly, her pulse pounding, her mind racing.

Kane was still pissed, and now she'd certainly been added to the list.

"Where's your dad?"

"Gone."

"I'm leaving, too." She paused and drew a bracing breath. "I'm not coming back."

"You agree with my father."

"Yes." And she was checking the weather report as soon as she got home, just to make sure hell hadn't frozen over. She was aligning herself with, if not the enemy, then certainly one of the few people she'd never understood.

"You're serious."

"We've worked too hard and too long for this championship to let it slip away now. If I leave, my dad will come back to the team, and you and your dad won't have anything to argue about."

He laughed, but he wasn't happy by any means. "My father and I have plenty to argue about."

"Maybe so, but I won't stand in the middle."

"You're really going to let them manipulate us like this?"

"I'm not being manipulated. I'm doing what's right."

"For the team."

"And for us." Standing one step above him, she prayed her hand would be steady as she laid it on the side of his face. "If we lost, we'd never forgive ourselves, or each other."

He stepped back, his rejection of her touch unmistakable. "So we're just going to break up every time we face a problem?"

"No, but this season is important."

"*Every* season is important."

"We're losing our crew chief over this!"

"This little thing. This *unimportant* thing. Funny, I thought our relationship meant more than that. I thought it was worth fighting for."

Was it? She wanted Kane, but she always felt as if he was just beyond her fingertips. "Are you sure you really want to be with me? Or did you just enjoy standing up to your father?"

"My father has nothing to do with us, beyond the fact that he's trying to stand between us and get his way. As usual."

"And you enjoy defying him."

"I'm just tired of him telling me what to do. He expects me to be someone I'm not, to be a PR darling, to pretend I'm not angry when I am, to be sorry I'm not the man he wants me to be."

And she wasn't the woman he wanted for his son. Whether Kane acknowledged it to her or himself that made a difference. There was a level of rebellion in his pursuit of her.

Besides, there was a vital element missing in their relationship.

"Do you love me, Kane?"

"I—" He turned away. "I'm not sure. I care about you. I want to be with you, and how do you know, *really* know about love?"

She knew, and at least now she also knew she was doing the right thing. She couldn't let him break her heart again. By her making the decision to end it, she could blame herself later instead of him. She could move on.

"We have a team meeting tomorrow at ten," she said as she moved past him.

"That's it? Business as usual?"

At the door she turned, forcing her face into a calm expression that was completely at odds with her emotions. "That's what racers do." And now what else did she have?

"I can't believe you're doing this," he said, stalking toward her. "You're giving up."

"I can't ask the team to sacrifice for me."

"Or me."

"For you, yes. For us, no. This is for the best, Kane. You know it is."

He grabbed her hand. "Lexie—"

She squeezed his hand, then stepped back. She couldn't touch him anymore and had to find some distance, or she wouldn't be able to function around him. "I'll always be here for you. But I just can't—" Her voice cracked. "I have to go."

He snagged her hand again and pulled her against him. She braced her palms on his chest, then jerked them back just as quickly. She couldn't stand this close to him, breathe his familiar scent, feel the heat of his body, and still do what she had to.

Being noble sucked big-time.

"Do you love me?"

She stopped breathing. She literally had to order her body to produce air.

Had she thought this was going to be easy? Had she believed Kane, competitive, fierce Kane was going to just nod and let her go?

Oddly, some small, desperate part of her was flattered. Which only made her decision more difficult to follow through on.

She did, though she chickened out on the actual words. She'd said them before, and they hadn't made any difference.

"I always have, and I always will."

KANE'S ARMS SLAPPED the surface of the water as he plowed his way across the pool.

He swam so he couldn't think, and prayed he wouldn't feel. He wasn't interested in reliving anything that had happened that day.

The memories intruded anyway.

You only started racing to defy me.

In the beginning, the secret of his racing had been an enticing draw. But eventually the rush of competition had overwhelmed that. Plus, he was good.

The quick reflexes he'd inherited from his father had served him well. And though his size had been a detriment on the football field, it had benefited his fit in a stock car. Disadvantages had become advantages.

I'm your father. I'm supposed to guide you.

Grudgingly he acknowledged he'd done that—in every other area besides sports. He'd taught him honor, loyalty, compassion and graciousness. And he'd shown him how to love a woman. How to treat a wife. A husband's devotion to his wife wasn't something every child got to see firsthand.

Maybe Kane hadn't always been understanding about the pressure his father was under, how hard it was to explain that his son hadn't wanted to follow in his footsteps.

A healthy dose of teenage ego and attitude certainly hadn't helped.

Regardless of his dad's good qualities, though, Kane needed to be free to live his own life. Part of him was relieved he'd unloaded his anger and frustration. He'd kept those feelings of never measuring up inside for too long. His delivery had been lousy and disrespectful, but he was still glad he'd said what he had.

Maybe the respect he longed for wouldn't be found in silence but in protest.

He dove underwater—deep, so his chest skimmed the bottom of the pool as he swam the length. His lungs burning, he surfaced at the shallow end, where the rock wall and fountain spurted recycled water. The gurgling noise was supposed to be relaxing. The designer had gone on and on about a Zen experience.

At the moment, the Zen was too quiet—probably the point. He needed noise, something to block out his conscience.

Are you sure you really want me? Or did you just enjoy standing up to your father for once?

Lexie's voice replayed in his head as he hoisted his body out of the pool. The cool fall air sent chill bumps racing across his skin. A welcome distraction.

Of course he wanted her, but he was furious and frustrated with her. He was furious and frustrated with himself.

Was he not enough for her? Was she choosing the team over him?

His ego and his anger assured him the answer to those questions was yes. He wanted her to devote herself to him, for him to be the center of her world and her attention.

On some rational level he realized she was in an impossible situation. The team her father had so painstakingly built was in jeopardy. She was being pulled in opposing directions. She wanted what was best for his career, but felt he couldn't be the best or have success when they were together. In his opinion, Harry and his father were exerting emotional blackmail. He wasn't going to fail or wash out of The Chase just because he and Lexie were together.

But once he set aside his ego, he knew he also had to examine his own actions. Had *he* devoted himself to *her*? Was she the center of his world?

He remembered thinking a few weeks ago that though he couldn't have his father's respect, he had Lexie's. Like he'd won her as a prize in a contest. Like one canceled the other. He couldn't confuse the two issues any longer. He wanted a better relationship with his father, but that was separate from his feelings for Lexie.

What *were* his feelings? How did he expect her to risk everything for him when he couldn't even say what he wanted? Or felt?

Somehow, even though he was a guy, he was pretty sure "I'm not sure whether you're the love of my life or not" weren't the words she was longing to hear.

Until he could figure out what he wanted, he had to suffer in silence.

His frustration over her choices wouldn't end, though. While his instinct was to stand his ground and prove them wrong, she chose to retreat. Why couldn't she see they didn't have to trade them for racing?

He wanted the NASCAR NEXTEL Cup Championship. He wanted it almost more than he wanted to draw his next breath. Endless breaks and sacrifices had gotten him to this point.

But he wanted more than racing. He wanted more than casual dates. He wanted a wife and a family. For so many years he'd thought those events were way off in a distant future, but now he was facing them.

Was the idea that he was even considering *wife* and

Lexie in the same breath proof enough? Or was she just someone familiar to fall back on? Was he just angry she'd dumped him—again—or was the pain in his chest something much deeper?

He couldn't seem to sort through it all.

"Kane!"

He winced at Cheryl's shout.

And I'm definitely not in the mood to deal with her.

"How did you get in here?" he demanded as she stalked toward him in a turquoise minidress and mile-high sandals.

She held up a key. "James."

And his buddy was going to catch major hell for sending the Powder Puff Mafia after him.

He snatched a towel off a lounge chair and wrapped it around his waist. "I'm not interested in company."

She cocked her hip. "No kidding?"

The woman was way too smart-alecky, and he had to admit he had a slight case of nerves at seeing her. Cheryl had a way of making people do things they never intended to do but did anyway because she just made them happen. He'd actually thought men were the only victims of this phenomenon until Lexie had told him about the ambush makeover Cheryl had pulled on her recently.

Truthfully, everybody at Hollister Racing was intimidated by their buxom office manager. He and James had flirted with her mildly when they'd first joined the team, only to have Cheryl inform them in brisk terms that she didn't date people she worked with. And besides, race car drivers—and their buddies—weren't anywhere on her list of turn-ons.

"I'm really busy," he said, scowling at her.

"Swimming."

"I'm an athlete. I need to exercise."

She rolled her eyes. "Convenient."

"Yes, it's convenient to swim in my own backyard rather than going to a gym."

"You do this daily, do you?"

How did she do it? *She'd* barged into *his* house, and he was already defensive and making excuses. "What do you want?"

"I'm so glad you asked...." She smirked, obviously pleased he'd given in to her demands so quickly. "You need to apologize to Lexie."

"Me?" he asked, incredulous and not pretending to understand how she knew the details of his love life mere hours after they'd occurred. "She's the one who broke up with me."

"Only because you forced her to."

"I didn't—"

"She dumped you because you were the greater risk."

"What's that supposed to mean?"

"You mean more to her than racing, but she understands racing better than she understands you."

"That's even less clear."

She spread her hands and smiled. "Hence, our conversation."

He dropped into a lounge chair and crossed his arms over his chest. If he was surly enough maybe she would go away. "We're not having a conversation."

"Not a very effective one, no."

"Because I don't want to talk—to you or anyone else."

"I realize that." She sighed. "But I'm an optimist."

"No, you're not."

Her hands planted on her hips, she glared down at him. "I'm trying, but you're making it awfully difficult. Back to my point," she added. "She's afraid to put her trust in you." She raised her eyebrows. "I can't imagine why."

"What's that supposed to mean?"

She rolled her eyes again. "And here I thought you'd catch on. I should have known."

"If you're pissed, you could leave."

"The easy way out," she said as she perched on the end of his lounge chair. "Something you should be familiar with."

"I—"

She raised a finger, and he fell silent. The woman was a witch, the way she commanded a room. Or, in his case, several acres of prime North Carolina real estate.

"How do you feel about Lexie?"

"That's none of your business."

She shook her head. "It's worse than I thought. You don't have Insensitive Male Syndrome. You just don't know, do you?"

A long silence followed. He was angry, tired and frustrated, but she was all he had. He couldn't imagine dissecting the female mind with James—his buddy knew less than he did.

He dropped his head into his hands. "I have no idea."

She patted his knee. "No worries. I'm here."

"But you scare me."

"Yes, I know." Standing, she paced beside his chair. "You like Lexie?" she asked after several minutes.

Confused, he looked up at her. "Of course I like her. She's a friend, a colleague. We grew up together."

"But we're not talking about your friendship. We're talking about love."

He swallowed. "Yeah."

"And we're not talking about the team."

"Right."

She raised her eyebrows, her gaze boring into his to the point he had to resist squirming. "You can do that? Separate the car chief from the woman?"

"I've got to, don't I?"

"Definitely." She resumed pacing. "So, racing aside, how do you feel when you're with her?"

He said nothing. This whole deal was beyond awkward.

"Please. I'm your therapist."

His mouth went dry at the thought. A therapist. A buxom blond therapist who—

Okay, there were worse things in life.

"I feel…fine."

"God help us."

"Okay, so maybe I feel great. I feel like I can conquer anything, like smiling is natural. I feel strong and important. I feel comfortable and safe, challenged and…"

"And?"

"Awed." He stared at the rippling pool. "I'm awed that she continues to be there for me, at how much she's helped me, after all we've been through, after all my shortcomings."

She was silent for so long, he finally looked up. "There's hope for you, Jackson."

"Oh, gee, is there really?"

"Surprisingly, yes. You communicate well?"

"We're attached by headsets at least three days a week."

She waggled her finger. "No racing."

"But we still—" he searched his mind for significant conversation that didn't involve racing "—talk," he finished lamely.

"And the physical communication?"

"I'm not going there with you, Cheryl."

"Well, she's never complained about any of *that*."

"No kidding."

"It's important, you know."

"No kidding."

She cleared her throat. "Okay, moving on…"

"Thank God."

"So, you…talk. About…something." She cut her gaze toward him. "Something complimentary about her would be good."

"I do that."

"Obviously not often enough."

"You're really getting on my nerves."

"Part of my job."

"Which I don't remember hiring you for."

She waved that technicality away. "So, you feel great around her, you have open communication and you want to be with her?" She glanced at him for confirmation.

"Yes."

"You're in love."

He surged to his feet. "Just like that?"

"You wanna argue?"

"I—"

"You've got a better conclusion?"

"A few simple questions and you know what I feel when I don't?"

"Actually I diagnosed you in about ten seconds." She waved her hand. "The rest was just so you wouldn't protest at my hourly rate."

"What rate?"

"Listen, buddy." She jabbed her fingernail into his bare chest. "You're not whipping your way through the water in fifty-degree weather because you're comfortable with your life and your decisions."

"The water's heated."

She glared at him. "You're emotionally bankrupt. You're lost in a sea of uncertainty, and only if she's with you will you find your true meaning in life. You need her like the flowers need rain and sunshine. She's warmth and hope. You long for her presence and will never feel complete until you have her by your side."

"I'm a guy, Cheryl. I can't possibly feel all that at once."

"Naturally. How could I forget?" She laid her hands on his shoulders and stared into his eyes as if she could communicate by the sheer force of her stare. "You're completely in love with that woman, but you have no idea what to do about it."

"I'm… Okay, well…" He lifted his chin. "Okay, maybe. It's possible. But how do I make her see I'm worth the risk?"

"I've got some ideas."

The fact that he was desperate enough to ask, "What?" proved to him he'd gone over the edge. Maybe the quick exit from the warm pool to the cool air really had stalled his brain functions.

"You've got to find a way to work through your feelings. To test them."

"How do I do that?"

She smiled.

CHAPTER FOURTEEN

"SIX RACES LEFT."

Shocked, Lexie glanced over at the man who'd dropped onto the barstool next to her.

Anton Jackson was nearly unrecognizable. She'd never been around him when a buzz of excitement didn't announce his presence in advance, but looking at him, she understood why. A dark cap was pulled low on his head, obscuring his artfully arranged blond curls. His posture was slumped. He was pale and unsteady.

"Buy you a beer?" he asked.

She shook her head in disbelief. She'd convinced James to drive her to a bar not too far from the speedway, but not high profile enough that she would draw attention. She wanted to be pathetic alone. "This is too weird."

"No kidding." He signaled the bartender. "Bud Light. You want a refill?" he added to her.

Lexie stared into her half-full martini glass. It was part of some weird, defiant, reminiscent confusion that stemmed from several weeks of personal and professional highs and lows that swung as wildly as a kid on a playground. The drink was too strong and too out of character.

But after a couple of them, they didn't taste too bad.

"Sure," she said, then drained the glass.

The bartender gave her a dubious look. "You're not driving anywhere, right?"

"No way." Her world was already blurry.

"He's been kind of erratic," Anton said after his beer was served.

"Kind of?" The last four races Kane had posted a second, a twenty-first, a third and a thirtieth. Other drivers in The Chase had also had a bit of trouble, so they were somehow hanging on to fifth. Coming into Talladega, the entire team was tired, frustrated and out of sorts.

Lexie was all that and more. She felt as if she was hanging on to her sanity and her job by a thread. Despite her and Kane's breakup, tension still filled her relationship with her father, though he hadn't quit. They were snappy and edgy. They rarely agreed, no doubt contributing to Kane's up-and-down performance.

"But he's still okay?" Anton asked.

"I have no idea."

"You work with him every day."

She sipped her drink, though she suddenly felt nauseous. "We don't really talk."

"Neither do we."

It was possible some of the blame for that was on her shoulders. She'd spent a lot of time lately telling Kane he shouldn't listen to his father, or try so hard to be like him. She'd advised him to be fierce and aggressive, instead of patient and amenable. But he'd gone so far to the aggressive side they'd been black-flagged for a lap last week.

Anton cleared his throat. "I'm, ah, sorry about barging in on you two that morning."

"It's okay. I've done plenty of things lately I'm not proud of."

"And I'm sorry if I've seemed critical of you and the team. I only want what's best for Kane."

"Since you know so much about what it takes to have a great race team."

"Not my biggest fan, are you?"

She wanted to squirm but instead she looked him in the eye. "No."

"I never gave you much reason to be. And that morning, I pushed way too—"

She waved away his apology. "You said what needed to be said. You were honest, which was more than I was doing. I knew I shouldn't be involved with Kane. I knew it would cause problems on the team, and I did it anyway."

"I should have kept my mouth shut. Your relationship wasn't any of my business."

She smiled weakly. "When's that ever stopped you?"

To her surprise he laughed. "Never, of course." He laid his hand over hers, and when she jolted, he held on. "I know we haven't always gotten along. That's mostly been my fault. I wanted Kane to focus on his career, not romance. And then there was the racing."

"I took him away from football."

"Yes, you did. I resented that for a long time. Truthfully, right up until that morning a few weeks ago. But that barrier is costing me my relationship with my son."

She wanted to argue, but she'd always felt that was a problem, so she didn't see how she could.

"It was convenient for me to blame you when Kane gave up football," Anton went on. "Convenient and wrong. I didn't want to see the truth—that my son didn't want to play football, that his heart was somewhere else. And not to spite me, or side with you, but just because that's who he is." He squeezed her hand again. "I have you to thank for that realization, Lexie."

"I didn't do anything," she mumbled, still bogged down in her own guilt. She could have been more understanding and less stubborn endless times in the past.

"But you did. If Kane hadn't been so busy defending you the other morning, if you hadn't been standing on his side, silently supporting him, he might never have told me off. I never realized he still felt so pressured to live up to my accomplishments. He might never have told·me how he really felt."

She'd helped Anton, and screwed herself up. *Terrific*.

"Do you love him?"

Her gaze darted to his. Truth time.

Like him, she'd come to some revealing conclusions over the past few weeks. The first of which was that her big plan to land a stable, ho-hum accountant and have a personal life outside of racing was a bust.

She loved this freakin' sport, and who else could understand her and her business but someone who was also consumed by it? Racing owned her—body and soul. Just like Kane.

"I was really hoping for an accountant but, yes, I do."

Either he realized she was half-drunk, or he didn't find anything odd about his son barely beating out an imaginary accountant.

"So why aren't you fighting for him?"

"I believed I was. I was being noble." She sighed in self-disgust. "Or so I told myself. If I've figured anything out in the last few weeks, it's what a big joke that is. I just didn't want to get hurt again. I didn't want to lose him again."

He raised his eyebrows. "The great Lexie Mercer scared to take a risk."

She lifted her hand. "Guilty."

"The greater the risk, the greater the reward."

"Is that supposed to be profound?"

"For a football player it is."

She smiled, and in seconds she was laughing. Anton joined her until the bartender stood in front of them, a concerned look on his face. "Do you two need a cab?"

"No." Anton tossed some money on the counter. "We've got a ride. Let's go," he said to Lexie.

"Are we actually going to come out of this as friends?" she asked as she gathered her purse and slid off the bar stool.

He grabbed her elbow when she swayed on her feet. "Stranger things have happened."

"I'm not so sure."

"I hope we can make it work, because I need a favor."

She blinked at him. "You didn't come for a beer?"

"I came for you. My car and driver are outside, waiting for us."

Sure enough, idling at the curb outside the bar was a big, black SUV with darkly tinted windows. A driver leaped out and opened the back door as they approached. Anton helped her inside, and Lexie could tell she was going to regret her martini experimentation in the morning. Next time she was sticking with her old standby—chocolate.

When Anton settled inside, he turned toward her. "I need you to help me get my son back."

"I HATE IT when I'm right," Lexie said the next morning, squinting into the bright sunlight on her way to the drivers' meeting.

Her father, walking beside her, snorted. "No, you don't."

Her temples pounded, and she slipped on a pair of sunglasses. "I do today."

"You were out pretty late last night."

She *really* needed to talk to Cheryl about not booking her and her father rooms side by side. "I guess so."

"I heard a man's voice."

"Yep. Anton Jackson."

Her father ground to a halt. "What?"

Laughing, she hooked her arm through his, forgetting for a minute that they were barely speaking. But when she started to step back, he pulled her into a hug. A quick one—they were in the middle of a busy path of crew members, media and officials, after all—but genuine enough that Lexie's heart felt lighter than it had in weeks.

"Come over here," he said, tugging her through the crowd to the alleyway beside the media center. "I'm sorry," he said, holding on to both her hands as they faced each other. "I've been a stubborn idiot the last few weeks. I left you and Kane in the lurch at Dover and threw off the team's focus. I've been grouchy and difficult." He squeezed her hands. "And jealous of him."

"Daddy, you're my number-one guy."

"I know." He looked down at the ground, then back up at her. His eyes were watery. "I've really enjoyed working side by side with you this year."

"We make a good team. Just like the old days."

"Yeah. I'm sorry I interfered between you and Kane. I was trying to protect you, and all I did was make you miserable."

"It's okay, Dad."

"Life is short. We know that better than most people."

Lexie's throat closed. She nodded as she blinked back tears.

"If he makes you happy, then you go for it."

"I plan to."

She never should have doubted Kane or given up on him, even with all the tension between her and her father and with all the possible consequences and doubts. The past few days, she hadn't been able to stop thinking about the race Kane had won at Bristol, how he'd refused to get out of the car until he spoke to her. He didn't do that to defy his father. He did that to show her she was important to him, that his win and his happiness weren't complete without her.

Her father pulled her into his arms and squeezed her tight. "I think your mother would have liked Kane."

"Me, too." She kissed his cheek.

"I have faith in you, sweetie. Kane, too."

"You should probably tell him that."

"I will."

Sniffling, they separated and looked around to make sure nobody had noticed they were crying on race day. And before the racing had even started.

"So…Anton Jackson?" her father asked as they walked through the garage area.

Lexie told him about the night before, about her and Anton bonding and forging a new friendship and about her promise to help father and son renew their relationship.

"He could start by coming to a race every once in a while," Harry commented, obviously not ready to forgive Anton so easily.

"He's here, isn't he?"

"We'll see how long it lasts."

Okay, so not every wall was going to come tumbling

down overnight. Since she was sure Anton was serious about this new commitment, she figured her father would come around eventually.

After the drivers' meeting, Kane retreated to his motor coach with James to relax as he usually did. Lexie watched him go with a sense of both anticipation and unease fluttering in her stomach. The past few days he'd stopped ignoring her and instead scowled at her constantly.

Two hours before race time, and the stands were already half-full. The grand lady at Talladega loomed like a mirage in the middle of the Alabama countryside. It was the biggest track on the circuit, with thousands of campers crowding the infield, and banking so steep you'd fall over if you tried to stand in the turns.

The drivers loved the speed. The fans loved the racing. The roar of the field as they came off the backstretch and into Turn Three sounded like a fleet of jets taking off. The barely controlled chaos during the race as cars went two, three, even four wide had fans holding their breath and hardly ever sitting in their seats.

Needless to say, Talladega wasn't the place for emotions, and their team had enough feelings flying around to satisfy Dr. Phil's schedule for at least a month.

There was too much to do before the race for her to waste time worrying. With the rest of the crew's help, she and her father organized the pit area, all the equipment and got the car into its place. By the time Kane and James strolled up, she had her car chief's hat firmly in place and had locked away her uncertainties.

And her assistant-for-the-day got the expected stunned reaction.

"Dad?" Kane asked when he reached them.

"Hey, son." Sweaty, his white polo stained with grease and wearing a team Sonomic Oil baseball cap and a broad smile, football legend Anton Jackson rocked back on his heels as if he was having the time of his life. "Lexie invited me to help out today."

Given the iciness between all of them, she'd taken a big chance by bringing Anton to such an important race. But there'd never be a perfect time. Racing wasn't going to stop so they could live. With all the drama this season, she'd learned that, if nothing else.

Kane turned his head toward her. "You invited him?"

"He came to the race on his own, and I didn't see any point in him standing on the sidelines."

Kane shrugged and turned away. "Whatever. As long as you people do your job, I won't have any problem doing mine."

Anton's smile faltered, but Lexie patted his shoulder. "Hang in there. He's always cranky before a race."

"Are you sure—"

"This is *my* pit, not his."

"No, I meant, are you sure you want him? He's got a serious ego problem."

Lexie grinned. "Like father, like son."

"Hey, I never—"

She crossed her arms over her chest.

"Okay, maybe he comes by it naturally."

"Come on, Mr. Hall of Fame," she said, guiding him toward the pit box. "I'll teach you the art of lap timing."

"HANG IN THERE," Harry said through Kane's headset. "Twenty laps to go. Run *your* race. Think ahead, and watch Lockwood's car."

Kane suppressed a stream of cuss words. "Lockwood? What now?"

"He sent his car chief down here to complain about you cutting him off."

The guy gave a whole new meaning to jerk. "Too bad."

"We need a top five out of this, so just keep your eyes open."

"How about a win?"

"Just dedicate it to me."

"You got it, boss."

Kane wasn't sure when it happened, but he and Harry were doing better. He still wasn't happy about what he considered his emotional blackmail of Lexie. But ultimately Lexie had made her own decision, and he had his own part in pushing her to it.

Later. Save it for later.

He pushed aside his frustration. He had plenty to say to her, as soon as the race was over. And he'd never wanted a race to be over so badly in his life.

At least Cheryl would be happy her plan worked.

"We got an offer from the sixty-three. He's going. You wanna go with him?"

"Let's do it."

With five laps to go, when the sixty-three car pulled out from their tight pack of seven cars, Kane followed him, putting his car millimeters from his back bumper and allowing the front car to pull him along in its wake. A couple of other cars jumped out behind him, and the whole line surged forward.

The sixty-three crossed the finish line first, and Kane sailed across just behind him.

"Great job, guys!" he shouted into the radio.

He pulled into his pit, then slid out of the car. After high fives from Lexie and the guys, he did the obligatory TV interviews, then rushed off to congratulate the winner.

On his way back to his hauler, he encountered Danny Lockwood.

"You cut me off."

With no intention of wasting one minute with this guy, Kane kept walking. "I drove through the giant hole you left open."

"I'm tired of having to deal with you."

"Too bad."

Lockwood shoved his shoulder. "I'm talking to you."

Kane stopped and turned. He'd dealt with his anger in productive ways—exercising, deep breathing and thinking through the consequences of giving in to his anger. He'd kept his cool through arguments with his father, nearly losing his crew chief and losing his girlfriend.

But he'd flat had enough.

"Get away from me," he said to Lockwood.

"Not until I have my say."

Blood roaring in his head, Kane clenched his fist and drew back. But before he could land the blow, Lexie jumped between him and Lockwood.

"Kane, no!"

"Get out of the way, Lexie."

She grabbed his arm and hung on. "No way."

"Let's go, son," his father said, laying his arm around his shoulders. "And I suggest you move along," he said to Lockwood with a piercing blue stare.

It wasn't easy, but Kane drew a deep breath and moved away with Lexie and his father.

"Need your daddy to fight your battles for you, Jackson?" Lockwood yelled after them.

As Kane turned back, one of his fans—dressed from head to toe in red and yellow Sonomic Oil/Kane Jackson gear—decked Lockwood.

Crew members and officials rushed toward them, some surrounding him, some surrounding the prone Lockwood. Kane was escorted to the NASCAR trailer, while Lockwood was taken to the infield care center.

He agreed wholeheartedly with the NASCAR big dogs that aggression and violence were no way to solve personal problems. With about twenty witnesses who saw him walking away, he figured he could afford to be magnanimous. NASCAR's president glared at him suspiciously, as if there might be a conspiracy between him and his fan.

Privately Kane vowed to pay all the fan's court fees if Lockwood pressed charges, and get him tickets and pit passes to any race he wanted.

When he left the trailer, his father was waiting for him. "Everything okay?"

Now that the excitement was over, the awkward tension between him and his father returned. "Probably. They said they'd give a final ruling Tuesday, but I don't see how they can blame me. I was walking away from the guy." He paused. "Uh, thanks for that, by the way."

"I was glad to help. I'm always here for you."

Kane stared at the ground. "Sure."

"Why don't I walk with you back to your coach?"

"Okay. I could really use a shower."

By moving quickly and ducking around the crowds, they managed to get to the drivers' compound with a minimum of stops for autographs. He guessed it was time to end the silence between him and his father, but he wanted to talk to Lexie even more.

After his shower, he found his father holding a bottle of Gatorade and pacing in the kitchen. "You want one?" he asked.

"Sure."

Anton pulled one from the fridge for Kane, and they stood just feet apart, each obviously waiting for the other to make the first move.

"Hey, thanks again for—"

"I didn't come to the Richmond race because of that newspaper article criticizing my support of your racing."

"I know."

"But it *was* a wake-up call for me. I've put too much emphasis on your image and how you're connected to me in the media. I've put too much distance between us because of my resentment of your racing. I truly never understood your fascination with the sport, mostly because I didn't want to. I wanted you to be like me, and you're not."

"I tried to be."

"I know, and I'm sorry you felt pressured to try. I'm sorry if anybody—including me—made you felt less than important because you were different." He laid his hand on his shoulder. "I'm so proud of you, of what you've done and what you're doing. Never again will you apologize to me or anybody else for doing what you love."

Relief and pride filled Kane. The equal footing he'd at least wanted a chance to share was there for him to enjoy. It would no doubt have been there sooner if he'd listened to Lexie and stood up to his father sooner. If he'd shared his frustration instead of bottling it.

He grinned and hugged him. "You got it, Dad."

After a few moments, his father pulled back slightly. "You be your own man, son. I'm here for advice whenever you need me, but I want you to do things your own way."

"You're not such a bad role model."

"I wanted to punch the crap out of that guy."

"Me, too," Kane said.

"Why didn't you?"

Kane grinned. "There was a time…" He shook his head. Obviously, he had grown up. "But mostly I was afraid."

"Of him?"

"No, of—"

"Lexie," they finished together.

"She's really something," his father added. "She told me if I didn't understand your love of racing it's because I never come to the races."

"And the ones you watch from the sky box don't count."

He smiled and nodded. "It's like you were there."

"I know her well."

"She's pretty terrific."

Kane raised his eyebrows. "She is, huh?"

"Because of her, I might actually get this racing bug. Which is good, because I'm cutting back on my broadcast schedule, so I can come to more races."

"Dad, you don't have to."

"I am. I've already told the NFL and the network. I'm going to alternate games with Buddy Romano."

"Your old center?"

"He's trying to break into TV, and I wanted some Sundays off. It seemed like the perfect compromise."

"And this was Lexie's idea?"

"She said I needed to take time with you and see what

NASCAR is all about. I need you to see that I'm serious about my commitment."

Kane sank onto the sofa. "Yeah, commitment."

"You don't want me to come to the races?"

"Yeah, I want you to come. I just—" He rubbed his hands down his face. "You had a good time today?"

His father sat beside him, and for the first time Kane noticed his rumpled, less-than-perfect appearance. "It was great." He looked off in the distance, as if reliving the day. "The speed, the power, the noise—it was all amazing. The air crackled like it was the Super Bowl."

"And it's that way every week."

"I can't wait. But what does this have to do with commitments?"

"Lexie." He said her name on a sigh, like the lovesick goofball he knew he'd become.

"Ah. Not ready to give up on her, are you?"

"No way."

"You shouldn't."

Though he and his father hadn't always agreed, Kane had always admired his parents' relationship. The respect and devotion they shared, which he understood even more because of his love for Lexie.

Love had hit him over the head, just as everybody had said it would. Although for him it had been more like a gradual fall, then an extreme plunge. Once, Lexie had said she loved him, too. But after all his uncertainty and indecision, his delaying, hemming and hawing, she'd probably changed her mind.

"Does love always make you crazy?"

His father patted him on the back. "Most of the time, son. Most of the time."

CHAPTER FIFTEEN

LEXIE MARCHED through the rapidly emptying drivers' lot, hoping she could still catch Kane.

They'd had a near miss with Lockwood but a great day on the track. She was proud of Kane pulling his punch, though she didn't want to consider what might have happened if she and Anton hadn't shown up. Still, the sight of that creep flat on his back had been worth the grilling in the NASCAR official's office.

Did Kane have the best fans or what?

As she reached his motor coach, she noticed a buxom blonde in a miniskirt standing at the door. *Oh, please.* She wanted to see Kane, to congratulate him and share the moment. To find a way to apologize for choosing the team over him. For chickening out. Protecting herself.

"Look, honey—" Her jaw dropped as she recognized the woman. *"Cheryl?"*

She waggled her manicured fingers. "Hi."

"What are *you* doing here?"

"I've been coming to the races the last few weeks."

"You *have?*" Cheryl didn't come to races. She didn't even *like* racing. "Why?"

"Kane and I…well, we've been working on a project."

Lexie's stomach bottomed out. Kane wouldn't. Cheryl wouldn't.

As if she realized her thoughts, Cheryl huffed in disgust. "Oh, please. *You're* the project."

"Me?"

"We've been trying to work through his feelings for you."

Despite her effort to be nosy and appropriately car chief concerned, her heart jumped. "Work through his feelings?"

"Well, see…" Cheryl stared at the ground in a very uncharacteristic way. "I thought he should compare the way he feels about you to the way he feels about racing."

Lexie shook her head to clear it. "Compare me to racing?"

"Yes. He was confused, and it was important that he get in touch with his emotions."

Good grief, not only was she destined to lose that contest, the woman was playing head games with a race car driver—the most volatile, superstitious, unpredictable species on the planet. "He was working out his feelings in a three-thousand-pound race car?"

"Where else would—"

"With forty-two other drivers also in three-thousand-pound race cars?"

Cheryl cocked one hip. "Men need something tactile to tap into their feelings. They're not naturally emotional beings like women."

"He was tactile all right—nearly on another driver's face. Do you have any idea what would have happened if that punch had landed?"

"It wouldn't have been good."

"No. The championship would have been lost." She snapped her fingers. "Just like that. NASCAR docks us twenty-five, maybe fifty points, and we're finished."

"Well, maybe—"

"Go home, Cheryl. Go back to running the office. Let me handle the team, the driver and the racing. Okay?"

"Jeez. I was just trying to help." She flipped her hair over her shoulder and stalked away.

Shaking her head, Lexie reached for Kane's motor coach door. She stopped with her fingers curled around the handle and looked over her shoulder at Cheryl. *"Did* he figure out his feelings about me?"

"He did."

"And?"

Cheryl nodded toward the door. "Why don't you go find out?"

Oh, she was just really too much. *Why don't you go find out?* Humph.

Comparing his feelings for her to his feelings for racing? How ridiculous. They were two completely separate—

Oh, they are, huh?

She swallowed. Hadn't she been the one who'd broken up with him years ago because she didn't want to be second best to his career? Then hadn't she, just a few weeks ago, broken off their relationship because she wanted racing to be first?

And she'd thought *he* was the volatile one.

Racing wasn't the problem. It was their hearts.

She'd let fears and insecurities convince her he didn't really love her. He'd focused so completely on proving himself to his father that his heart didn't have room to give her the devotion she needed.

They wouldn't repeat the mistakes of the past. The bruising her heart had taken had healed, and she wasn't afraid to hand it over to the man she loved.

She flung open the door to the coach. "I l—" She ground

to a halt when she saw the other two men with Kane. "Hi, Dad, Anton."

While the two older men rose to their feet, the love of her life looked a little green around the gills as he stared silently up at her from his position on the sofa. "Are you okay?" she asked him.

"I'm—"

"On your feet, son," Anton said, grabbing Kane by his arm. "There's a lady in the room."

"Don't nag the boy, Jackson," her father said.

Anton narrowed his eyes. "So only the crew chief can nag him, is that right?"

Her father poked out his chest, which was no match for the size and breadth of the former NFL great. "That's right."

"He's my son."

"At the track he belongs to me."

"Hey, guys," Lexie said.

"Dad, please," Kane said at the same time.

The two men separated, leaving Kane and Lexie standing between them. Well, at least they weren't standing on opposite sides anymore.

"I came to apologize to Kane, and he—" her father jerked his thumb at Anton "—had the nerve to tell me all the problems I caused by not supporting you two."

Lexie bit her lip to keep from laughing at the haughty expression on Anton's face. "Ah, Dad, there were some problems—"

"No more than *he* caused," her father said, glaring at Anton.

"You *both* were wrong," Kane said, sounding tired, as if he'd said that a few times already. "We've talked about this. You've both apologized. Several times."

"He can be so pompous," her father said. "I'm going to make it my mission to stamp it out of my grandkids."

Kane's jaw dropped. *"Grandkids?* Aren't we getting a little ahead of ourselves?"

"Well, now this whole misunderstanding…" Anton began, though Lexie tuned him out. She was listening to a louder voice, one deep inside her.

Go for it.

Lexie wrapped her arms around Kane's neck. "You don't belong to either of them. You belong to *me*. At the track. Everywhere."

He hugged her tight against his chest, his eyes glowing with relief. "Lexie, I've made such a mess out of things."

"Nothing that can't be fixed, right?"

"Now we're talking," her father said, looking proud. "See, I told you she loved him."

"No, I told you," Anton said, shaking his head.

"Would you people get out of here?" she said, glaring at their fathers. "So *I* can tell him I love him?"

"Apologies accepted," Kane said, never taking his gaze from Lexie's. "Bye."

Within seconds she and Kane were alone, and he was kissing her.

"You wanna run that last part by me again?" he asked when he came up for air.

"I love you."

"And always will?"

She smiled. "Always. And you—"

"Did you see Cheryl?"

Where was he going with this? Where was the big declaration of love from him? "Ah, yeah."

"Did she tell you about the plan?"

"Uh-huh."

"She's crazy." He shook his head. "She had me doing all this deep breathing."

"And you had some terrible finishes."

"Yeah." He grinned. "You gotta keep your head in the race at all times."

Wait a second. This *was* going somewhere. "You risked championship points for *me?*"

"I'd do anything for you." He cupped her cheek. "You should know that by now."

Okay, that was really flattering and gave her all kinds of warm, fuzzy feelings. But at the same time…

"Are you crazy?" She fought the urge to pull her hair out, then his. "We've got a championship to win. Races to run. Not to mention the safety of—"

"I had more important things on my mind."

"No kidding?"

His gaze smoky, he kissed her. "Like telling Cheryl of course I loved you, and she should go home and quit bugging me."

Her stomach fluttered. "You do, huh? When did you realize that?"

"About twenty seconds after I met you."

She raised her eyebrows. "And the last twelve years, you've been…"

"Stupid. I guess I should confess that more recently I knew I loved you when, at every race since you walked out of my house, I haven't wanted to get in the car. I wanted to stay with you. I didn't give a damn what lap we were on or where we stood in the points. If I can't be with you, race with you, I don't want to race at all."

The fluttering in her stomach blossomed, sending

tingles of happiness through the rest of her body. It was a feeling she knew would last a lifetime—for both of them. "You don't have to pick between me and racing."

"I don't?"

"You can have us both."

"Mmm." He kissed the side of her neck. "Can I have you first?"

"You bet. And just so we're clear, I didn't choose the team over you. I chose to protect myself rather than risking my heart again."

His gaze searched hers. "You won't be sorry if you do."

"No, I don't think I will," she said, and pressed her lips to his.

They shared a kiss full of hunger and need, healing and hope. She absorbed his excitement and relief. His hope and promise.

There would be hard days ahead, working together and loving together, but she had faith in their commitment to each other. A love this challenging to win would be all the more precious.

The alarm on her watch beeped. She pulled away from Kane and glared at her wrist. "Oh, crap. We've got to head to the airport. We'll miss the plane."

Grinning, he pulled her back to him. "I was thinking about staying the night."

"CAN YOU SEE ANYTHING?" Harry asked, hovering impatiently behind the taller man in front of him.

"They're kissing," Anton said, turning away from the window with a broad smile on his face.

"Again?"

"In fact, I don't imagine we'll see them on the plane."

Harry sagged with relief. "Hallelujah."

Anton dropped his arm across Harry's shoulders as they walked away from the coach. "Not a bad plan, Mercer."

"Not bad? It worked perfectly."

"I think they would have gotten back together without us fighting."

"Eventually, I guess. But it was taking too dang long. I've got a championship to win."

"Did I ever tell you about that touchdown I made in Super Bowl—"

"If you don't finish that sentence, I'll buy you a beer."

Anton nodded. "Deal."

EPILOGUE

KANE WON THE RACES in Charlotte and Martinsville. He came in second in Atlanta and third in Texas. So, by the time they reached Phoenix, they were in first place.

Tonight, with a fifth-place finish at Homestead, they locked up the championship—and Lexie gained a fiancé.

Kane refused to hoist the NASCAR NEXTEL Cup trophy until Lexie accepted his marriage proposal. As soon as he climbed out of the race car he went down on bended knee in their pit box in front of their family, entire crew and millions of TV viewers, and asked the woman he loved to be his wife.

Of course she said yes.

Two celebrations began.

Lexie knew she'd leave the wedding to the experts—Cheryl and James—and simply be grateful for what she had. A man she loved more every day and whose devotion she felt constantly in return, a father who supported her both on and off the track, future in-laws who had amazing perspective and class and a championship they'd all won together.

"When do we get to escape all this attention?" Kane whispered in her ear in the alternate Victory Lane NASCAR had set up for their championship celebration.

"I told you to finish below twentieth, then we could have run off to a hotel on the beach."

"A beach hotel with my lovely car chief or win the championship?" He angled his head in consideration. "It was a touch choice."

"Next hat!" the photographer shouted, so everyone on the team moved to the next sponsor's hat.

"But you're getting both."

"I am?"

"I made reservations. A week at a resort in the Bahamas. We leave the moment I can pull you away from the congratulations brigade."

"I love you."

"I know. I love you, too. Smile for the camera."

During the break between pictures, James leaned across her to ask Kane, "I get to be best man, don't I?"

"Who else?"

"No wild bachelor parties," Lexie said sternly. "Our champion has to say in fighting shape. We defend our title in thirteen weeks."

Exchanging a smile, Kane and James upended a bottle of champagne over her head.

* * * * *

Mediterranean Nights

Join the guests and crew of Alexandra's Dream, *the newest luxury ship to set sail on the romantic Mediterranean, as they experience the glamorous world of cruising.*

A new Harlequin continuity series begins in June 2007 with FROM RUSSIA, WITH LOVE by Ingrid Weaver.

Marina Artamova books a cabin on the luxurious cruise ship Alexandra's Dream, *when she finds out that her orphaned nephew and his adoptive father are aboard. She's determined to be reunited with the boy…but the romantic ambience of the ship and her undeniable attraction to a man she considers her enemy are about to interfere with her quest!*

Turn the page for a sneak preview!

Piraeus, Greece

"THERE SHE IS, Stefan. *Alexandra's Dream*." David Anderson squatted beside his new son and pointed at the dark blue hull that towered above the pier. The cruise ship was a majestic sight, twelve decks high and as long as a city block. A circle of silver and gold stars, the logo of the Liberty Cruise Line, gleamed from the swept-back smokestack. Like some legendary sea creature born for the water, the ship emanated power from every sleek curve—even at rest it held the promise of motion. "That's going to be our home for the next ten days."

The child beside him remained silent, his cheeks working in and out as he sucked furiously on his thumb. Hair so blond it appeared white ruffled against his forehead in the harbor breeze. The baby-sweet scent unique to the very young mingled with the tang of the sea.

"Ship," David said. "Uh, *parakhod*."

From beneath his bangs, Stefan looked at the *Alexandra's Dream*. Although he didn't release his thumb, the corners of his mouth tightened with the beginning of a smile.

David grinned. That was Stefan's first smile this afternoon, one of only two since they had left the orphanage yesterday. It was probably because of the boat—according to the orphanage staff, the boy loved boats, which was the main reason David had decided to book this cruise. Then again, there was a strong possibility the smile could have been a reaction to David's attempt at pocket-dictionary Russian. Whatever the cause, it was a good start.

The liaison from the adoption agency had claimed that Stefan had been taught some English, but David had yet to see evidence of it. David continued to speak, positive his son would understand his tone even if he couldn't grasp the words. "This is her maiden voyage. Her first trip, just like this is our first trip, and that makes it special." He motioned toward the stage that had been set up on the pier beneath the ship's bow. "That's why everyone's celebrating."

The ship's official christening ceremony had been held the day before and had been a closed affair, with only the cruise-line executives and VIP guests invited, but the stage hadn't yet been disassembled. Banners bearing the blue and white of the Greek flag of the ship's owner, as well as the Liberty circle of stars logo, draped the edges of the platform. In the center, a group of musicians and a dance troupe dressed in traditional white folk costumes performed for the benefit of the *Alexandra's Dream*'s first passengers. Their audience was in a festive mood, snapping their fingers in time to the music while the dancers twirled and wove through their steps.

David bobbed his head to the rhythm of the mandolins. They were playing a folk tune that seemed vaguely familiar, possibly from a movie he'd seen. He hummed a few notes. "Catchy melody, isn't it?"

Stefan turned his gaze on David. His eyes were a striking shade of blue, as cool and pale as a winter horizon and far too solemn for a child not yet five. Still, the smile that hovered at the corners of his mouth persisted. He moved his head with the music, mirroring David's motion.

David gave a silent cheer at the interaction. Hopefully, this cruise would provide countless opportunities for more. "Hey, good for you," he said. "Do you like the music?"

The child's eyes sparked. He withdrew his thumb with a pop. *"Moozika!"*

"Music. Right!" David held out his hand. "Come on, let's go closer so we can watch the dancers."

Stefan grasped David's hand quickly, as if he feared it would be withdrawn. In an instant his budding smile was replaced by a look close to panic.

Did he remember the car accident that had killed his parents? It would be a mercy if he didn't. As far as David knew, Stefan had never spoken of it to anyone. Whatever he had seen had made him run so far from the crash that the police hadn't found him until the next day. The event had traumatized him to the extent that he hadn't uttered a word until his fifth week at the orphanage. Even now he seldom talked.

David sat back on his heels and brushed the hair from Stefan's forehead. That solemn, too-old gaze locked with his, and for an instant, David felt as if he looked back in time at an image of himself thirty years ago.

He didn't need to speak the same language to understand exactly how this boy felt. He knew what it meant to be alone and powerless among strangers, trying to be brave and tough but wishing with every fiber of his being for a place to belong, to be safe, and most of all for someone to love him….

He knew in his heart he would be a good parent to Stefan. It was why he had never considered halting the adoption process after Ellie had left him. He hadn't balked when he'd learned of the recent claim by Stefan's spinster aunt, either; the absentee relative had shown up too late for her case to be considered. The adoption was meant to be. He and this child already shared a bond that went deeper than paperwork or legalities.

A seagull screeched overhead, making Stefan start and press closer to David.

"That's my boy," David murmured. He swallowed hard, struck by the simple truth of what he had just said.

That's my *boy*.

"I CAN'T BE PATIENT, RUDOLPH. I'm not going to stand by and watch my nephew get ripped from his country and his roots to live on the other side of the world."

Rudolph hissed out a slow breath. "Marina, I don't like the sound of that. What are you planning?"

"I'm going to talk some sense into this American kidnapper."

"No. Absolutely not. No offence, but diplomacy is not your strong suit."

"Diplomacy be damned. Their ship's due to sail at five o'clock."

"Then you wouldn't have an opportunity to speak with him even if his lawyer agreed to a meeting."

"I'll have ten days of opportunities, Rudolph, since I plan to be on board that ship."

* * * * *

*Follow Marina and David as they join forces
to uncover the reason behind little Stefan's
unusual silence, and the secret behind the death
of his parents....*

Look for From Russia, With Love
*by Ingrid Weaver
in stores June 2007.*

REQUEST YOUR FREE BOOKS!

2 FREE NOVELS PLUS 2 FREE GIFTS!

 Silhouette®

SPECIAL EDITION®

Life, Love and Family!

YES! Please send me 2 FREE Silhouette Special Edition® novels and my 2 FREE gifts. After receiving them, if I don't wish to receive any more books, I can return the shipping statement marked "cancel." If I don't cancel, I will receive 6 brand-new novels every month and be billed just $4.24 per book in the U.S., or $4.99 per book in Canada, plus 25¢ shipping and handling per book and applicable taxes, if any*. That's a savings of at least 15% off the cover price! I understand that accepting the 2 free books and gifts places me under no obligation to buy anything. I can always return a shipment and cancel at any time. Even if I never buy another book from Silhouette, the two free books and gifts are mine to keep forever.

235 SDN EEYU 335 SDN EEY6

Name	(PLEASE PRINT)
Address	Apt.
City	State/Prov.	Zip/Postal Code

Signature (if under 18, a parent or guardian must sign)

Mail to the **Silhouette Reader Service™**:
IN U.S.A.: P.O. Box 1867, Buffalo, NY 14240-1867
IN CANADA: P.O. Box 609, Fort Erie, Ontario L2A 5X3

Not valid to current Silhouette Special Edition subscribers.

Want to try two free books from another line?
Call 1-800-873-8635 or visit www.morefreebooks.com.

* Terms and prices subject to change without notice. NY residents add applicable sales tax. Canadian residents will be charged applicable provincial taxes and GST. This offer is limited to one order per household. All orders subject to approval. Credit or debit balances in a customer's account(s) may be offset by any other outstanding balance owed by or to the customer. Please allow 4 to 6 weeks for delivery.

Your Privacy: Silhouette is committed to protecting your privacy. Our Privacy Policy is available online at www.eHarlequin.com or upon request from the Reader Service. From time to time we make our lists of customers available to reputable firms who may have a product or service of interest to you. If you would prefer we not share your name and address, please check here. ☐

SSE07

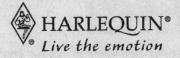